FREDDY
and
SIMON
the
DICTATOR

The Complete FREDDY THE PIG Series
Available from The Overlook Press

Please inquire about special prices on a complete set (or sets) of the original twenty-six Freddy books—for individuals or for library donations. Call 1-800-473-1312

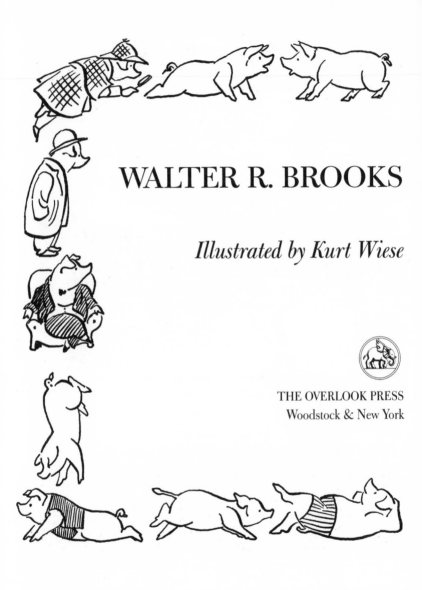

WALTER R. BROOKS

Illustrated by Kurt Wiese

THE OVERLOOK PRESS

Woodstock & New York

FREDDY *and*

SIMON *the*
DICTATOR

If you enjoyed this book, very likely you will be interested not only in the other Freddy books published in this series, but also in joining the *Friends of Freddy,* an organization of Freddy devotees.

We will be pleased to hear from any reader about our "Freddy" publishing program. You can easily contact us by logging on either THE OVERLOOK PRESS website, or the Freddy website.

The website addresses are as follows:
THE OVERLOOK PRESS:
www.overlookpress.com

FREDDY:
www.friendsoffreddy.org

We look forward to hearing from you soon.

First published in the United States in 2003 by
The Overlook Press, Peter Mayer Publishers, Inc.
Woodstock & New York

WOODSTOCK:
One Overlook Drive
Woodstock, NY 12498
www.overlookpress.com
[for individual orders, bulk and special sales, contact our Woodstock office]

NEW YORK:
141 Wooster Street
New York, NY 10012

Dust jacket and endpaper artwork courtesy of the Lee Secrest collection and archive.

Cataloging-in-Publication Data is available from the Library of Congress.

Brooks, Walter R., 1886-1958.
Freddy and Simon the dictator / Walter R. Brooks ; illustrated by Kurt Wiese.
p. cm.

Manufactured in the United States of America
ISBN 1-58567-359-5
1 3 5 7 9 8 6 4 2

FREDDY

and

SIMON

the

DICTATOR

CHAPTER

1

"Look, Freddy, you dope," said Jinx, the black cat; "what do you want to learn to lash your tail for? You're not a cat. You're a pig. And, strictly speaking, you haven't really *got* a tail, anyway."

"Oh, is that so!" said Freddy. "Well, I've

got enough of a tail so that when I wanted to learn to wag it, like a dog, I got Georgie to teach me, and I learned to wag it in two lessons. Look!"

It wasn't really much of a wag; it was more of a tremble; but Jinx, watching carefully, could see that the pig's tail did move. "Very pretty," he said. "But why are you always trying to do something that pigs can't do? Remember when you hired that squirrel to teach you to climb trees, and you got two feet off the ground and fell and sprained both fore trotters? Tail lashing is not for pigs."

"I know, Jinx," said Freddy mournfully. "But you handle your tail so elegantly. It's a real pleasure to watch you. Of course I wouldn't expect ever to be as graceful as you are, but don't you suppose you could give me some exercises, maybe, so my tail could be a little more expressive?"

Cats are vain animals, and Freddy knew that he could get Jinx to do almost anything by paying him a few compliments on his handsome figure or his gentlemanly manners. Now the cat had difficulty in hiding his pleasure. He suppressed a purr and yawned instead, covering his mouth delicately with one paw. Then he said: "Yes, we cats are naturally graceful; it's not something you can learn. But I suppose— yes, I think I could do something for you. But your tail's kinked up so tight. If you could manage to straighten it out—"

"It only straightens out when I'm scared," Freddy said.

"That's no good," said Jinx. "H'm, Mrs. Bean is ironing today. We might go down to the house and have her press it out straight with a hot iron."

"Not on your life!" said Freddy. "Not *my* tail. Well, I guess—" He stopped as a high thin squealing and sobbing broke out on the other side of the cow barn, in front of which they were standing. "What on earth—!"

"One of the rabbits," said Jinx. "Sounds like he's caught in a trap. Come on."

But at the edge of the vegetable garden, they saw that the rabbit wasn't in any trap, he was across Mr. Bean's knee, getting spanked. And a second rabbit was held tightly under Mr. Bean's arm, waiting his turn. He was making almost as much noise as the first one.

Mr. Bean looked up and nodded to Freddy and Jinx but went right on spanking. At last when he had spanked the second rabbit, he let

them both go and they ran off, hobbling and
pretending to be crippled for life, and when
they got to what they felt was a safe distance,
they stopped and turned around and made faces
at the farmer. "Yaah, yaah, yaah!" they yelled.
"You big bully! You wait—we'll get even with
you for this!" And so on.

Freddy shook his head. "Never saw any
animal on this farm talk back to Mr. Bean before," he said.

But Mr. Bean paid no attention to the jeers.
"Told 'em next time I caught 'em stealing lettuce I'd spank 'em, and I did," he said to
Freddy. "Don't know what's got into the rabbits—they've been gettin' into all kinds of mis-
chief lately. Broke two windows in the wood-
shed Friday. Throwing stones. And pulled half
Mrs. B's washing off the line. Might think they
was tigers instead of rabbits. Though I'm glad
they ain't. Wouldn't care to spank a tiger." And
he made the fizzing sound that meant that he
was laughing behind his beard.

Mr. Bean didn't usually talk much to his
animals, even to Freddy. He was kind of old-
fashioned, and it was hard for him to get used
to the idea that animals could talk. It embarrassed him to talk to them, or to have them an-

swer. Freddy knew that he must be pretty upset about the rabbits to have said so much. So he said: "I know those two. They're Numbers 6 Jr. and 14." There were so many rabbits on the farm that they had been given numbers instead of names. "I'll talk to their mothers."

"Do that," said Mr. Bean, and he whacked Freddy on the shoulder and turned and went down to the farmhouse.

Jinx said: "Those two are Horribles, aren't they?"

Freddy nodded. The Horribles, otherwise the Horrible Ten, had been organized as a joke by a group of rabbits. With their ears pinned flat to their heads, and brandishing daggers cut out of tin, they would lie in wait after dark for some animal and then rush out and dance a sort of war dance around their victim, chanting one of their bloodthirsty songs. "I don't know what's getting into the Horribles," Freddy said. "Mr. Bean has had several complaints about them. At least everybody thinks it was them that broke into Miss McMinickle's house down the road and raided her icebox, and the next night threw stones at Mr. Margarine's car."

"Well," said Jinx, "I suppose after you've

jumped out and scared everybody you know a dozen times, it kind of loses its point. You want to go on to bigger and better things."

"But not stealing things, for goodness' sake," said Freddy, "and destroying property."

"Why don't you talk to 23. Or 12. They've done detective work for you, and they're both good steady boys. I'll bet they haven't been in on any of this rough stuff."

"Let's go talk to 6 Jr.'s mother first," Freddy said.

So they went on up to the upper pasture where Mrs. 6 lived in a comfortable burrow not far from the duck pond. Mrs. 6 had eight children, two of whom, 6 Jr. and 62, were Horribles. Freddy called down the hole which was Mrs. 6's front door, but nobody answered, and he and Jinx were turning away when a rabbit came hopping up.

"Hello, 23," said Freddy. "You're just the rabbit I want."

"Well, here I am," said 23. "Got a job for me?"

"Not exactly," said the pig. "But I think maybe you can tell me what's gone wrong with all you Horribles. I've had some pretty bad reports about you lately, and Mr. Bean just caught 6 Jr. and 14 stealing lettuce again. What are you doing, trying to work up a crime wave?"

23 looked embarrassed. "I—I know. There's been a lot of things. But I hope you don't think I was in on any of them."

"No, I didn't think you were, or 12 either. That's why I'm asking you what it's all about."

The rabbit hesitated. "I don't want to be a tattletale," he said. "And besides, I don't think it would be very healthy for me to tell you all I know—or guess. On the other hand, as a loyal citizen of the First Animal Republic . . ." He broke off. "Oh dear," he said, "I wish—I wish I could tell you, Freddy, but I don't see—"

Jinx sprang forward and, with his paws on his shoulders, shook him until his teeth rattled. "Come on, you pink-eyed powder puff," he said, "let's have it. Give."

"Hold it, Jinx," Freddy said. "You won't get anything out of 23 that way. He's a good boy, and loyal to Mr. Bean. Isn't that right, 23? He'll tell us."

"O.K., pig; have it your way," said the cat. "Me, I'd tie him up and tickle his toes until he spilled everything he knew. But you go ahead and see how far your soft-soaping him will get you."

"It'll get farther than rough stuff," said Freddy. "Look, 23. We don't want you to give away any secrets that you've promised not to. Just tell us what you can, honorably."

The cat laughed sarcastically. But 23 said: "You can find out almost as much as I know, Freddy, without my telling you anything, if you'll go up to the Grimby house tonight after dark. Don't get too close; there'll be a lot of animals there and if they see you—well, you won't find out much."

"You mean there's some kind of a meeting there?" Freddy asked. The Grimby house in the Big Woods had burned down two years ago, and there was nothing left but a cellar hole half filled with charred beams and other debris. It was here that Freddy's lifelong enemies, the rats under old Simon, had made their last stand against the animals of the Bean farm.

"I don't want to tell you any more," 23 said. "I'd be in serious trouble if it got out that I'd said anything to you. But I'll say this, Freddy: If later on, you decide to do anything about it, there are a few of us you can count on. There's 12 and 24. And 18 and 34. One or two others." He hesitated. "Well . . . I guess that's all for now. Be seeing you around." And he hopped off.

"Say, what *is* this, Freddy?" said Jinx. "A conspiracy or something? You suppose these rabbits are planning to overthrow the government?"

"Maybe we'll find out tonight," said the pig. He turned to bow politely to an elderly rabbit who was coming slowly towards them. "Good afternoon, Mrs. 6. We were looking for you."

To his surprise, the rabbit, who had always in the past been very pleasant to him—had indeed seemed flattered to be spoken to by so important a member of the barnyard group—frowned and eyed him coldly. "I have nothing to say to you," she said, and moved towards her front door.

Freddy blocked the way. "Please, Mrs. 6," he said. "I want to talk to you about 6 Jr. He's always been a good boy, but just recently some of these younger rabbits have been running wild, and I want to see if we can't find some way to straighten them out. Just today 6 Jr. and 14 were caught by Mr. Bean stealing lettuce, and —"

"You needn't go on," said Mrs. 6 coldly. "I know all about that. As brutal an attack as I ever saw! Beating up two helpless little children!

Well, your fine Mr. Bean will get his comeuppance—you wait and see. Why can't he pick on someone his own size?"

"Probably because nobody his own size was stealing his property," said Jinx.

But Freddy said: "Hold on a minute! You say you saw Mr. Bean spanking 6 Jr.? Then you were there. You mean you just stood by and watched them stealing lettuce without trying to stop them?"

"I not only didn't try to stop them, I told them to take the lettuce. And what are you going to do about that, Mr. Smarty Pig?"

"Well, I'll be darned!" Jinx muttered. He and Freddy stared at each other, hardly able to believe their ears. That a responsible mother of a family would actually urge her child to steal was incredible.

Jinx was the first to recover himself. "Hey!" he exclaimed. "You're the one Mr. Bean ought to have spanked. By gosh, I'll do it for him." His paw shot out and caught Mrs. 6 by the shoulder.

But Freddy stopped him. "Wait a minute," he said. "We must get to the bottom of this. Mrs. 6, will you tell me why you turned against Mr. Bean, who has always been kind and considerate to all the animals on the farm?"

She held out a piece of paper to Freddy.

"Tell you?" said Mrs. 6 angrily, "indeed and I'll tell you! It's the same reason why I'm left a poor widow woman with eight fatherless children. It's your fine Mr. Bean that's responsible for that."

"Oh, come," said Freddy. "I was on that case, when your husband disappeared two years ago. There wasn't a clue—certainly nothing to connect his disappearance with Mr. Bean. He just walked out one night and vanished."

"And who's to blame him?" said Jinx, looking distastefully at Mrs. 6. "Got sick of being nagged at, and just up and went over the hill. Smart guy, if you ask me."

"Oh, sure," said the rabbit. "I know that's what some people said. But Mr. 6 wasn't nagged; we never had a cross word. And why was nothing ever seen or heard of him again? Why didn't you, Freddy, find any trace of him? I'll tell you why. You wait here." She hopped into her front door.

In a minute, she was back. She held out a piece of paper to Freddy. It was a leaf torn out of a cookbook. "Rabbit stew," Freddy read. "Cut up your rabbit and place him in a saucepan . . ."

"Sure," said the rabbit. "Cut up Mr. 6— that's what your kind, sweet Mrs. Bean did.

Fried him and had him for supper. How do I know? Because that's a page out of Mrs. Bean's cookbook, that's how!"

"Where'd you get this?" Freddy asked. "Even if it *was* out of Mrs. Bean's cookbook, I wouldn't believe that the Beans had your husband for supper. I don't know anybody but Jinx, or the mice, or probably the two dogs, who could get into Mrs. Bean's kitchen to tear a page out of her cookbook. Where'd you get it?"

"I'm not at liberty to say," Mrs. 6 replied.

"I thought so," said Freddy. "Somebody has done this to set you—and if they can, all the other rabbits—against the Beans." He thought a minute. "Well," he said finally, "I'm not going to argue with you. If you're silly enough to believe that, you're too silly to argue with. Come on, Jinx."

CHAPTER

2

Two years earlier, Freddy had driven the rats
out of the Grimby house cellar, where they had
dug themselves in, by dumping a lot of spoiled
onions in the cellar hole. Rats don't even like
fresh onions, and spoiled ones make them very
sick. Shortly after this, as has been related else-

where, all but one of the rats had been shipped out to a ranch in Montana. Freddy was sure that that time he had got rid of them for good.

Since then, he hadn't visited the Grimby house. As he and Jinx crept up towards it through the woods that evening, there was no taint of spoiled onions in the air. Two years of rain and snow and sunshine had taken it all away.

Jinx was all black, and even in the daytime could have slipped through the woods without being noticed. But though Freddy was a skilled woodsman, and could move as silently as a shadow, he knew that he was too pale in color to escape attention, and so he had put on one of the many disguises he used in his detective work: a black morning coat, gray striped trousers, and a derby hat. With this, and a dark false beard to hide his face, he was nearly invisible.

They sneaked up as close to the ruined house as they dared. It was not very close. For they sensed, rather than heard, the presence of a large gathering of animals. There was no talk; everyone was keeping very quiet; but there were rustlings, whisperings—and then suddenly a great voice came roaring out of the cellar hole.

"Attention, friends! At our last meeting, you

learned something of the true nature of the human race, and particularly of your masters, Bean and Witherspoon, Macy and Schermerhorn, the farmers on whose land you live and whose slaves you are. For make no mistake, friends, slaves you are, ruled by whip and gun. This very afternoon, one of the most brutal punishments ever suffered by any animal was inflicted upon two helpless young rabbits by Mr. William Bean. Beaten within an inch of their lives, they were left moaning and half dead beside the vegetable garden where they had been innocently nibbling at a wilted lettuce leaf.

"But enough of this, friends. I am not here tonight to tell you of these things. Every one of you knows of the wrongs and cruelties he himself has suffered at the hands of these men. Every one of you bitterly resents the oppression which he is powerless to overcome."

A small shrill voice cut across the speaker's roaring tones. "Mr. Bean is kind to his animals."

"I know that he has that reputation," came the reply. "I know that he *says* he is kind to them. And no doubt to some of them he does show kindness at times. A horse or a dog will work harder for a kind master than for an unkind one. But is it kindness to beat young rabbits into insensibility? Is it kindness to make a stew of the father of a large family and serve him up for supper? No, friends, such kindness is not what we have a right to expect."

Jinx put his mouth close to Freddy's ear. "Something familiar about that voice," he muttered.

"Is to me, too," said the pig. "But only one of the cows would have as big a one. Like Mrs. Wiggins when she gets to laughing."

" 'Tisn't a cow," said Jinx. "Look, I'm going to climb a tree and see if I can get a squint at the guy. I want to see who's here, too. This business could be serious."

How serious it could be, Freddy was to learn later. Now he listened as the big voice went on. "I said a moment ago that we animals were powerless. As long as we are each of us acting alone, that is true. One animal by himself can do nothing. But suppose ten thousand animals, on the farms about Centerboro, banded together in the cause of freedom! Suppose ten million animals in New York State! Friends, in one night we could cast off our chains! We could take over these farms—yes, and the villages, too, and later, even the cities. We could run them for ourselves, for the workers who are today deprived of the fruit of their labors by their masters, the farmers.

"Many of you, I know, will find it hard to think of humans as your enemies. You have lived beside them in peace for generations. But there was peace only because you submitted to their rule. What happened when you rebelled? What happened to the rats, the one group of animals who never submitted to the Beans and their like? You are told that rats are hateful, sly, and vicious; that they are thieves and out-laws. But who tells you that? The farmers. And why? Because the rats chose to be free, to take orders from no human. For what is their crime? To take a little grain from the farmers' store—grain which grows on the land, and which should be free to all. And for that they were chased and shot at, driven out into the woods like criminals, and finally exiled to Montana.

"But enough of this. I have shown you what we must do. If we wish to live free lives, in a free country—to do as we please, rather than as Mr. Bean or Mr. Witherspoon pleases—then we must organize. That is a matter which I will take up at our next meeting. In the mean-while, think over what I have said, consider carefully what you wish to do. If you wish to continue living as slaves, then I am wasting my time here. But if you have the will to burst your shackles and enter into the glorious life of free animals, then I will show you the way.

"Now, are there any questions?"

For a moment there was silence. Then the small voice which had spoken before—it was a rabbit's, and Freddy thought it was 12's—said: "Why don't you tell us who you are?"

"Who I am," was the reply, "will be revealed in due course. This, I will tell you: I am not a human."

"You a bug?" the little voice asked.

There were a few faint snickers, but it is a measure of the seriousness with which the listeners took the speaker that there was no laughter. This, as much as anything that had been said, worried Freddy. If the farm animals were taking this creature, whoever he was, seriously, there was big trouble ahead.

Freddy decided that he had learned all he needed to, and he thought he had better leave before the meeting broke up. He backed out of the bush where he had taken cover and sneaked off down through the woods.

When he got to the pig pen, Freddy didn't go straight to bed. He didn't even take off the derby and the morning coat, but sat down in his big chair and put his feet up on the desk beside the old typewriter on which he composed his poems and prepared the copy for his weekly animal newspaper, the Bean Home News. He wanted to think.

He was still thinking, to the accompaniment of good hearty snores, an hour later when Jinx tapped at the door, then pushed it open, and came in. Seeing his friend asleep, the cat grinned, tiptoed up close to him, and suddenly screeched: "Arise, pig! Cast off your chains! The revolution has dawned! The animals have taken over!"

Freddy arose all right. He went right up out of the chair as if he were on springs, and before his eyes were open, grabbed a stick from the corner, dashed to the door, and throwing it open, assumed an attitude of defense. Then his eyes opened and he began to relax. "Dawn?" he muttered. " 'Tisn't dawn yet. Black as your hat out."

He stood there for a second or two, then turned and saw Jinx. "Darn you, cat," he said crossly, "I wish you'd quit these silly jokes." He picked up the derby, which had fallen to the floor, and brushed the dust off it tenderly. "I was just thinking—" he began.

"Arise, pig!"

"Boy, I'll say you were—thinking on all twelve cylinders," said Jinx. "Could hear you all the way down from the woods."

"Yeah," Freddy said. "Very comical. But suppose you tell me what you saw."

"I didn't see much," said the cat seriously. "I know we're supposed to see in the dark, and we can, better than most animals. But not in the pitch-black, the way it was there. Matter of fact, owls can see better in the dark than cats can.— Hey, how about that screech owl pal of yours, the one that swallowed the dictionary—Uncle Solomon? I bet he knows what's going on."

"Probably Old Whibley does, too," said Freddy. Whibley was a big owl who lived with his niece, Vera, in a tree not far from the Grimby house. "We'd better see him tomorrow."

"I didn't see the speaker," Jinx went on, "though I waited nearly an hour after they all left. Nobody came out of the cellar. There were some big animals in the audience, though. I saw a couple of horses, and at least one cow; and I gathered that there were some skunks there—I don't know whether it was Sniffy Wilson and his family or not. Mostly, though, they were just small animals. Lots of rabbits."

"Well," said Freddy, "my guess is that whoever's behind all this doesn't really hope to take over New York State for the animals, much less the whole country. Nobody would be so foolish as to propose that. But suppose he keeps up this talk about how cruel and mean Mr. Bean is—twisting things that happen like spanking the rabbits. First thing you know, he'll have 'em believing that Mr. Bean *is* mean and cruel, and ought to have his farm taken away from him. And a bunch of animals *could* drive a farmer off. Remember how Mr. Anderson and the rats drove Mrs. Filmore away from her summer hotel?"

"I wonder why he spoke of the rats," said Jinx. "That didn't go down very well."

Freddy said: "I don't know. Thank goodness the rats are gone. There was only one, Eli, that didn't get shipped off to Montana. Simon sent him on an errand and he didn't get back till the rest had gone. But he's living quietly in Tushville. I've seen him once or twice at the movies in Centerboro. He walks over. Has a private entrance somewhere under the stage, he told me, so he doesn't have to pay admission."

"I don't see how anybody could stir up trouble for Mr. Bean among the animals," said the cat. "Witherspoon, yes; he's stingy. They say he won't even let his barn cat have table scraps."

"There aren't any, that's why," said Freddy. "Not after he and his wife get through. You know his horse, Jerry, told me that often for dinner, he and his wife divide a fried egg, and then give the cat the shell to lick.

"But as far as stirring up trouble for Mr. Bean, it wouldn't be hard. By now, Mrs. 6 has peddled that recipe for stewed rabbit all over the farm, and ninety per cent of the rabbits believe that the Beans had old 6 for supper. Although all of 'em know that he ran away because he couldn't stand his wife's nagging, and wanted peace and quiet. Besides which, he'd have been tougher'n an old boot."

"We've got to stop this thing before it goes too far," said Jinx. "Let's get some of the old crowd together and bust up their next meeting, hey?"

"And suppose some rabbit gets a black eye. Can't you hear them all hollering cruelty again? No, this has to be handled carefully." Freddy suddenly yawned uncontrollably. "All this thinking," he said—"takes it out of me. Must get my rest or I'll be no good in the morning."

"You sure aren't much good tonight," said Jinx. "Haven't you any ideas at all?"

Freddy took off the morning coat and hung it on a hanger. "What have I been passing out to you for the last hour?" he demanded. "You can't recognize an idea when you see one. Look, cat; who are the enemies of the Bean farm? First there's Herb Garble, and his sister, Mrs. Underdunk. Then there's Mr. Anderson, the real estate man. And then Simon and his gang of rats. They've all tried, singly or working together, to get the farm away from the Beans. But I think Garble is the worst. He doesn't just want the farm; he hates us; he'd like to burn us at the stake or boil us in oil or something. Anderson doesn't hate us; he'd just like to do the Beans out of the farm. As for the rats—well, they're just rats. Anyway, all but one of 'em are in Montana."

"You think Garble's behind this, then," said Jinx.

"He's the likeliest one. And remember, he owns the Big Woods—bought 'em from Mr. Margarine." Freddy got a clean nightshirt out of a drawer and pulled it on over his head. "So even though that wasn't Garble's voice tonight, he's the one we ought to check on first." He pulled back the covers and got into bed. "Well, good-night, Jinx. Want to stay? Curl up in the armchair."

"With all those broken springs poking up into me? Thanks," said the cat. "I'd rather

curl up on a hot griddle. See you in the morning, pig."

But Freddy was already asleep.

CHAPTER

3

Mr. J. J. Pomeroy was a robin, and the head of the A.B.I., the Animal Bureau of Investigation, which often worked with Freddy on his detective cases. The next morning, Freddy called on Mr. Pomeroy in his nest in the elm tree on the Bean's front lawn. That is, he didn't try to climb up to the nest; he tapped on the tree trunk, and Mr. Pomeroy flew down to him.

After they had exchanged greetings and Freddy had inquired after the health of Mrs. Pomeroy and the children, he told Mr. Pomeroy about last night's meeting.

"Dear, dear," said the robin, "I don't like the sound of that."

"Neither do I," Freddy said, "and I think you'd better put your whole force on it right away. I'd watch Garble and Anderson. We know they're enemies of the Beans, and of the F.A.R."

"I'll do it right away," said Mr. Pomeroy. "I know there's been something going on— some unrest, specially among the rabbits, but I couldn't put a claw on it. Only it certainly isn't just the rabbits. I agree with you that there's probably a man behind it. But we'll— Hey!" he broke off. "Look who's coming."

A long black car was turning through the gate. It stopped beside Freddy, and a short red-faced man with a bristly mustache leaned out of the window. "Hi, Freddy!"

"Mr. Camphor!" Freddy exclaimed, and went over and shook hands.

"Why so formal?" Mr. Camphor asked.

"What's the use of having a first name if your friends won't use it?"

"I'm sorry—er, Jimson," said the pig. "May I present my friend, Mr. J. J. Pomeroy? He's head of the A.B.I. Mr. C. Jimson Camphor, J.J."

The robin flew up into the window opening and extended a claw. "Very happy to meet you, sir. I've heard a good deal about you, of course."

"And you're going to hear more, I'm afraid," Mr. Camphor said. "You know what I've done, Freddy? I've let 'em persuade me to run for governor of the state."

"Why, that's wonderful, Jimson," said Freddy. "I'm sure you'll make a good one."

"Cheer up," said Mr. Camphor gloomily. "Maybe I won't get elected. Goodness, I don't know anything about governing. Oh, I've worked in Washington a lot, on committees investigating things. But when Senator Blunder and Judge Anguish and some of 'em came and asked me to run—well, all I could think of was that I'd be famous, and I said yes. So I got nominated on the Republican ticket. But then I got to thinking I didn't know anything about being governor, and maybe my fame would be the wrong kind—you know what the newspapers would say: 'Governor Camphor's administration has been marked by the most abjectly stupid incompetency ever exhibited by an incumbent of the gubernatorial mansion.' Stuff like that."

"Guber—what?" inquired Mr. Pomeroy.

"It's Latin for governor," said Freddy. "Anybody can use words like that ought to get elected easy. That one word alone ought to be good for ten thousand votes. And 'incumbent'—easily another five thousand."

"That's the trouble," Mr. Camphor said. "When I'm in front of an audience, I just can't help using words like those. I could sound like a fine governor, if I didn't have to do any governing. Freddy, you've just got to get me out of this. And you've had political experience. Electing that cow—your friend Mrs. Wiggins—as President of the First Animal Republic. Come up for a few days. The committee's there now, planning the campaign. You can tell 'em confidentially that I'm a crook or something—not fit to sit in the governor's chair."

Freddy shook his head. "They won't listen to a pig."

"You won't be a pig; you'll be a local politician—Dr. Hopper. The same disguise you had when we had the trouble with Mr. Eha, remember? Sure, a doctor—you can tell 'em I'm crazy—not fit to govern. And that's true enough, anyway." Mr. Camphor frowned and was silent a moment. "There's something else, too," he said. "A detective job. Just came up last night, and— Well, I'll tell you when you get there. I do need you, Freddy."

Even though he was needed badly at home, Freddy didn't see how he could refuse. Mr. Camphor was a close friend, and had done him many favors. He gave Mr. Pomeroy certain instructions, and then went up to the pig pen, and put on the black clothes and the derby and the beard he had worn the previous evening. Then he glanced at himself in the mirror and frowned. He looked enough like a human to get by, if the lights weren't too bright. He had found that people usually see what they expect to see. Introduced to Dr. Hopper, they'd see Dr. Hopper. He might look like a pig, but it wouldn't occur to them that he really was one. But in the house he'd have to take the derby off and he couldn't get by without a hat on.

He didn't like wigs. They always looked false. Beards nowadays, even real ones, looked false anyway, so the beard didn't matter. He opened the wig drawer in his dresser and tried on several, finally selecting a very curly one that came well down over his forehead. Then with the scissors he trimmed the beard to a point, to look more professional.

"By George, Freddy," said Mr. Camphor, as the pig got into the car, "you certainly do look distinguished. You're the one ought to be running for governor—not me." He thought a minute. "I wonder if we couldn't arrange it. I wonder—"

Freddy didn't say anything. He didn't know much about politics, but he thought it highly unlikely that even the most powerful political machine would dare to put a pig into such an important position. They drove down the Centerboro road, and after a mile or so, swung left into the road that led up to the south shore of Otesaraga Lake. A few miles farther, and the car turned through the tall iron gates of the Camphor estate.

On the terrace in front of the big house, a group of distinguished-looking men were sitting in garden chairs. They were all smoking large cigars, and seemed to be having a lively argument.

"Oh dear," said Freddy. "Jimson, I—I don't think I'll be any good here. I can't dis-

Finally he selected a very curly one that came well down over his forehead.

cuss high government affairs with these people."

Mr. Camphor laughed. "If you did, they
wouldn't know what you were talking about.
You sit still and listen for a while; I guess you
can get into the conversation all right. When I
left, they were arguing about the best way to
make fudge." He took Freddy out on to the
terrace and introduced him. "My friend, Dr.
Hopper, gentlemen. Senator Blunder, Judge
Anguish, Colonel Buglett, Mr. Slurp, Mr.
Glockenspiel." They shook hands. "Dr. Hopper is my chief political adviser," Mr. Camphor said.

"Never heard of him," said Colonel Buglett
shortly.

Freddy scowled. He still felt out of place,
and would have been happy to sink through the
flagging of the terrace, if there had been a
trap door handy. But he was angry at the rude-
ness offered to Mr. Camphor. He drew himself
up. "Never heard of you, either," he said.

Colonel Buglett scowled too and started to
his feet, but Judge Anguish put a hand on his
arm. "Come, come, Percy," he said; and then
to Freddy: "I'm sure Colonel Buglett didn't
mean any discourtesy."

"No discourtesy," said the Colonel. "Just meant I never heard of him."

Freddy and Mr. Camphor both opened their mouths to speak, but Senator Blunder stood up and raised his hand. "Gentlemen," he said commandingly, "the party can never elect a governor if we are continually snapping at one another. I had never heard of Dr. Hopper either until Mr. Camphor spoke of him yesterday. But I have every confidence in Mr. Camphor's judgment; if I had not, I would scarcely wish to have him as governor of our great state. Therefore, when Mr. Camphor tells us that Dr. Hopper is a truly great politician, I accept that statement as the truth."

Colonel Buglett still looked doubtful, but before he could say anything, Mr. Camphor said: "I should perhaps have given you a little more information about Dr. Hopper's experience and background. Perhaps if I say that he was formerly adviser to President Wiggins, it will be enough. No one, I suppose, will care to question President Wiggins' fame."

Apparently no one did, but Freddy could see all of their lips moving as they tried to place Wiggins in the long list of Presidents of the United States. He could actually read the lips of some of them. Colonel Buglett started at the present and worked backward. He got as far as Harding and stuck. Senator Blunder and Mr. Slurp worked from the other end. With their heads together, they were whispering: "Washington, Adams, Jefferson, Madison . . ." They got as far as Buchanan before they bogged down.

Mr. Glockenspiel asked what Wiggins was doing now.

"*General* Wiggins," said Mr. Camphor. "Commander in Chief of the F.A.R." He spoke as if he were shocked that Mr. Glockenspiel could be so ignorant.

Freddy had a hard time keeping a straight face. Of course, his whiskers helped a lot. He wished Jinx was there, to hear all this. Actually, everything Mr. Camphor had said was the truth, but if these men had known that the Wiggins, whose name they were hearing with such respect, was a cow . . . And the F.A.R., the First Animal Republic on the Bean farm . . . But, of course, there were so many government departments and labor unions and organizations of various kinds that were known only by their initials—like the C.I.O. and the N.A.M. and so on—that politicians couldn't possibly keep track of them all. But they wouldn't dare ask and thus expose their ignorance. Probably, they thought the F.A.R. was the Federal Army Reserve, or something like that.

Whatever they may have thought, they didn't seem to have any more doubts about Dr. Hopper. Mr. Camphor's bluff had turned him into a very important person. Freddy decided that a little more bluffing wouldn't do any harm. "Gentlemen," he said, "I should perhaps tell you at once that General Wiggins and I had a long conference yesterday on the possibility of electing Mr. Camphor governor. And though this may come as a shock to some of you—and particularly to you, Jimson—the General will not support your candidacy."

Now if you are told that some piece of information will come as a shock to you, the chances are that you will really feel shocked, even if the information itself isn't of the slightest importance. Senator Blunder said: "Good gracious me!" and Mr. Slurp threw up his hands. Even Colonel Buglett seemed put out. Mr. Camphor, however, did not make a success of his expression. It is hard to look disappointed with a broad grin on your face.

Judge Anguish said: "This is very strange. What seems to be the General's objection?"

"Well, gentlemen—" Freddy hesitated. "This is confidential, you understand. The General would be very indignant if it leaked out to the newspapers. He does not question Mr. Camphor's ability. But he feels—and I think perhaps, on due consideration, you will agree with him—that no governor should yawn continually through the speeches of members of his own party. Or on other public occasions. I regret to report this, Jimson, but you know yourself that during General Wiggins' Fourth of July speech last year, you expressed boredom rather than enthusiasm."

"Dear me," said Mr. Camphor, "did I really? But of course I *was* bored. Nine out of ten political speeches are just a lot of hot air. Good gracious, even my own speeches bore me to death. I can hardly keep awake to finish them."

"Very damaging admission," said Colonel Buglett.

"I don't see it," said Mr. Camphor. "I should think the audience, being bored too, would feel sympathetic towards me."

Judge Anguish said: "Political speeches are

not supposed to say anything important. The perfect political speech expresses a lot of noble but very vague sentiments in extremely high-flown language. That's what brings out the votes."

Freddy thought of the flowery speeches that his friend Charles, the rooster, made, and of the enthusiastic applause they brought out, although ten minutes after Charles had finished, nobody could remember what he had said.

"General Wiggins had several other objections," Freddy went on. "He said that he esteemed you highly as an assistant, but that there were several things about you that made you undesirable as a figure who must appear dignified on public platforms and on public occasions. The General mentioned specially that at a rally in Syracuse you slapped two babies instead of kissing them—"

"Of course I slapped them," said Mr. Camphor. "When I started to kiss them, they bit me."

"He also said," Freddy went on, "that he felt that your habit of eating gumdrops in public was highly undignified. Particularly, when someone in the audience asks you a question, and you can't get your jaws apart to answer it."

"I have always eaten gumdrops," said Mr. Camphor. "I am very fond of gumdrops. Particularly the licorice ones. If I have to give up gumdrops in order to become governor, then I renounce the honor. As to dignity, I have never pretended to be dignified. When dignity is needed, I summon my butler. That is what I hire him for. Bannister!" he called.

A very tall man in a black coat with tails came out of the house and crossed the terrace to stand beside Mr. Camphor's chair. He was so dignified that he didn't look at Mr. Camphor; he held his head up very high and looked out across the lake. "You rang, sir?" he asked.

"I yelled," said Mr. Camphor.

"Just so, sir," said Bannister.

"We need a little dignity, Bannister."

"Yes, sir," said the man. "Thank you, sir." And he continued to stand staring out superciliously over the water.

"By George!" Senator Blunder exclaimed. "You really haven't much dignity, Camphor. I never realized it before."

"It's what I've been telling you," Mr. Camphor replied. "I'm not fit to be governor."

"Now, now," Judge Anguish interrupted, "you promised, Camphor. And it's too late to change now. Why, we've got the ballots all printed with your name on them. Do you realize what that costs?"

"And there's no reason why you can't lay off gumdrops, at least in public, for a while," put in Mr. Slurp.

"He can't lay off giggling," said Freddy. "That's the thing that seemed most serious of all to General Wiggins. It doesn't matter whether he's addressing the legislature or laying a cornerstone—he giggles all the time. Even in church, he giggles. The General says we don't want a giggling governor."

"Certainly not," said the Judge. "But is that so, Camphor? I hadn't noticed that you giggled."

"Oh, yes," said Mr. Camphor. "Can't seem to help it, somehow. At the solemnest moments. Te-hee! There I go now. Hee-hee-hee!" He giggled violently.

"Good gracious!" Senator Blunder exclaimed. "This is serious! I'm glad we found it out. Still . . . Camphor's the man we want. Isn't there some cure for it—can't something be done, Dr. Hopper? We can keep him away from babies, and we can make him promise to swear off gumdrops. Can't you give him some treatment for these giggles?"

Before Freddy could reply, Bannister suddenly spoke. He didn't move, and his eyes still looked off across the lake. "Laugh and the world laughs with you," he said.

Freddy remembered how fond Mr. Camphor and Bannister were of proverbs. They were always arguing about them, and testing them out to see if they were true. Now Mr. Camphor stopped giggling. "Maybe you're right, Bannister," he said, "but it isn't so that giggle and the world giggles with you. The world just thinks you're silly."

"Dear me," said Mr. Slurp; "what do you think, gentlemen—it's pretty late in the day to drop Camphor from the ticket, but after all—a giggler!"

"Not dignified, no," said Judge Anguish. "But perhaps there's been too much dignity in government. *We* like it. But do the people like it? You know, gentlemen, I have a hunch that they'd like a little less dignity and more giggles. Yes, gentlemen, that gives me an idea. The first new idea in politics in a hundred years. There's our slogan: 'Laugh and the world laughs with you.' And instead of making the usual speeches, all full of campaign promises, Camphor will tell jokes and giggle. Camphor, the giggling governor! It's a natural, gentlemen. It will be a landslide!"

"I believe you're right, Anguish," said the Senator; and Colonel Buglett said: "You've got something there." Mr. Slurp and Mr. Glockenspiel nodded approval.

"Shucks!" said Mr. Camphor disgustedly. He looked up at Bannister. "Oh, go away," he said. "You and your dignity!"

The committee had gone into a huddle. Each one had a favorite joke that he was trying to suggest for Mr. Camphor's speeches, and each was laughing so hard at his own joke that he heard nothing the others said. Bannister glanced at them, then bent down. "He who laughs last, laughs best," he said. He winked at Freddy, whom he had, of course, recognized, since he had seen the Dr. Hopper disguise before. Then he bowed stiffly and turned and marched into the house.

CHAPTER

While the committee were roaring and laughing at their jokes, Mr. Camphor motioned Freddy to come down to the other end of the terrace.

"What do we do now?" he asked. "My goodness, it gets worse and worse. Now I'm not only going to be governor, I'm going to be a giggling governor."

The pig said he was sorry. "They were the best things I could think of offhand. Don't worry, Jimson. I'll think of something." So he thought for a minute.

Mr. Camphor could see that he was thinking, because he shut his eyes and put on a fiercely determined look. But when presently he opened his eyes, he shook his head. "No good," he said. "Thinking's like fishing. You bait your hook and throw it in the water, but if there aren't any fish around, you naturally can't catch anything. There isn't an idea around anywhere right now. I'll try again later."

So Mr. Camphor sighed and said: "Well, come in the house then; I want to show you something."

In the living room, a lady was sitting by the window, reading. She was rather fluttery looking; there were little ribbons all over her dress, and as she read, her hands kept moving and fluttering, and she nodded, and pursed her lips, and laughed a little tinkling laugh all the time as if she were trying to entertain a visitor instead of reading a book.

"Miss Anguish," said Mr. Camphor, "may I present Dr. Henry Hopper? This is the Judge's sister, Miss Lydia Anguish, Henry."

Miss Anguish jumped up, and the book fell on the table, and several bits of ribbon floated off her dress. "Oh, dear me," said Miss Anguish; "how very interesting! Not Henry Hopper, the distinguished movie actor?" And she reached out to shake hands. She held her hand so high up that Freddy had to stand on tiptoe to take it.

"Movie actor? . . . No," he said. "Is there a Henry Hopper in the movies? I don't remember seeing him."

"Oh, I don't know," she said, and gave a tittering laugh. "You *look* so much like a distinguished movie actor that I just thought that you—well, that you must be one. And then if you were, why then your name would be Henry Hopper, because that is your name."

"Er—yes, so it would," said Freddy. Then he repeated, "So it would," because he couldn't think of anything else to say. He glanced sideways at Mr. Camphor, but Mr. Camphor was looking up at the ceiling, with his mouth pursed as if about to whistle. Then Freddy caught sight of himself in the mirror. There was certainly nobody in the movies who even remotely resembled what he saw—unless it was one of the dwarfs in Snow-White.

Miss Anguish was looking expectantly at him but he couldn't think of anything else to say. To conceal his embarrassment, he picked up the book she had dropped. He was surprised to see that it was one of the series of books in which his own adventures had been related by a Mr. Brooks, the official historian of the Bean farm, who occasionally came out and spent a week or so at the farmhouse.

"Such an interesting book," said Miss Anguish. "Have you read it? All about animals that talk. Imagine!"

Mr. Camphor's eyes came down from the ceiling and he said: "It's all true, too. I know those animals; the pig, Freddy, is quite a friend of mine. He lives only a few miles from here."

"Oh come, Jimson—really!" said Freddy. "You mustn't expect us to believe that stuff."

"What's so incredible?" said Mr. Camphor. "You can talk; pig can talk. He's rather your build too, Doctor. If you'd like to see him and talk to him, Miss Anguish, I'll drive you down someday. Maybe he'd recite some of his poetry for you."

"A poetic pig!" Miss Anguish exclaimed. "What won't they think of next!"

"You oughtn't to talk like that, Jimson," said Freddy, when they had gone through into the dining room. "Somebody'll get on to me if you aren't careful."

"That one wouldn't get on to anything if you dressed up that horse of Bean's in a toga and introduced him as Julius Caesar. If she didn't quite see the likeness, you could point out that Hank has a Roman nose. Oh, probably I shouldn't have done it, Freddy, but I couldn't resist it; you look so darned funny in that outfit. . . . Oh dear, I hope I haven't hurt your feelings!"

"It isn't me you're laughing at—it's the disguise," said Freddy. "I'd probably laugh at you if you were disguised as a pig. I'd be sore if you laughed at my looks when I didn't have the disguise on, though."

"I guess people only look ridiculous when they try to look like something they aren't," said Mr. Camphor. "Whether it's false whiskers they put on, or just a very noble and heroic expression. Like that rooster friend of yours when he makes a patriotic speech. He's probably patriotic all right, but his speeches are just too patriotic to be true.

"But here, Freddy, this is what I wanted to show you." He opened a drawer in the sideboard and took out a white handkerchief. It had the initials W.F.B. embroidered in one corner. "Those are Mr. Bean's initials, aren't they?"

"Sure. It's his handkerchief."

"I was afraid so. Well, Freddy, five hundred dollars was stolen last night from the top of the dresser in Senator Blunder's room, and this handkerchief was found on the floor in front of the dresser. Now in the first place, if Mr. Bean was going to rob my house, he wouldn't be foolish enough to leave his handkerchief behind. And in the second place, Mr. Bean is an honest man and wouldn't rob my house anyway." He hesitated a minute. "I guess I didn't need that part about the first place, did I? However, Senator Blunder doesn't know Mr. Bean, and he wanted to call the police in right away. But I persuaded him to wait a while."

"How did he know the initials were Mr. Bean's?" Freddy asked.

"He went through all the B's in the Centerboro phone book till he found somebody they fitted. I told him I knew Mr. Bean and I was sure he was too busy on his farm to go in for burgling, and I said he was a good party man and had always voted for Senator Blunder—did he, do you know, Freddy?"

"Have no idea."

"Well, let's hope he did. Because it wasn't until I said that a headline in all the papers—Prominent Republican Jailed for Theft—might have a bad effect on the election, that he agreed to wait a few days. But I had to promise that if I couldn't find the thief and get the money back, I'd make up the five hundred myself. So I hope you can find the thief, Freddy. But I guess it'll be quite a job. You don't really think it could be Mr. Bean, do you?"

"It wasn't Mr. Bean," said the pig. "This handkerchief proves it."

"My gracious, it would prove it *was* Mr. Bean to a policeman. Of course, Mr. Bean is our friend, and we know he doesn't go round burgling houses; but I don't see how his leaving his handkerchief here proves that he doesn't."

Freddy said: "Look at the handkerchief. It's clean. But it hasn't been ironed. What does that tell you?" And when Mr. Camphor just looked blank, he went on. "It tells you that Mr. Bean didn't drop it there. Because when Mrs. Bean does a washing, she hangs it on the clothesline, and when it's dry, she takes it in and sprinkles it and irons it, and puts it away. There's no way that Mr. Bean would get a clean handkerchief but by going to his bureau drawer and getting one that had been ironed. Unless he took an unironed one off the line, and Mrs. Bean wouldn't let him do that.

"But there was somebody that took a handkerchief off the line the other night. A bunch of rabbits deliberately pulled Mrs. Bean's clothesline down, and some things were stolen."

He went on and told Mr. Camphor about the trouble on the farm and the mysterious speaker at the Grimby house meetings, who was trying to stir up the animals to revolt and take over the farms from their human owners.

"You know," he said, "this sort of thing has been tried before. Remember when Mr. Anderson and the rats drove everybody out of that summer hotel across the lake and took it over? And tried to scare the Beans out of their house? And the time that woodpecker came and made himself dictator, and tried to build an animal empire out of the F.A.R.?

"But this seems to me more serious. This time somebody's trying to set the animals against the humans, make an animal empire in which the humans will work for the animals, instead of the other way round. It won't work, of course. The humans will win out in the end. But there'll be an awful lot of trouble if we can't break it up here, before it gets started."

"It's a long way from stealing Blunder's money to building an empire," said Mr. Camphor. "And the idea of a rabbit burglar is almost as incredible to me as a rabbit emperor."

"Well, for one thing," Freddy said, "whoever is stirring up all this business isn't a rabbit, I'm sure. And the burglar wasn't necessarily a rabbit, either. There were lots of other animals at that meeting. Couldn't a squirrel have got in the Senator's window last night?"

"The window was open. I suppose he could. But the important thing is to get the money back. Do you think you can, Freddy?"

"It'll be a job. My guess is that the burglars had two objects in stealing the money: to put some cash in their war chest, and to start stirring up trouble among the humans. That's the way the Communists do; they go into a country and get everybody fighting everybody else, and when the whole country is in an uproar, they step in and seize the power and anything else that isn't nailed down. And the way this speaker up at the Grimby house is talking to the animals is the Communist way. Tell a big lie, and the first time, nobody believes it much. Like the Beans having rabbit stew. But keep repeating it, and by and by somebody says: 'I wonder if maybe they *did* have rabbit stew!' And then it's

*A bunch of rabbits deliberately pulled Mrs. Bean's
clothesline down.*

told and repeated so often that everybody comes to believe it."

"Well, my goodness, Freddy," Mr. Camphor said, "I think you ought to go back home and put a stop to these revolutionists. That is much more important than my little troubles. I'll get out of being governor some way. No, no; you go on back. And if in the course of your work you do find the money—well, I'll be very grateful."

But Freddy shook his head. "There's nothing much I can do right now," he said, "that the A.B.I. can't do better. It's a question of getting more information about whoever runs these meetings. And about—oh, a lot of things. I can just as well stay up here for a few days and let Mr. Pomeroy gather the facts for me. Because we can't take any action until we know a lot more than we do now about who's back of this business. And in the meantime, we can work out some scheme to get the committee to withdraw your name from the ticket."

"My goodness, if giggling won't make them drop me, I don't know what else we can do. How silly can a governor get?"

"I'll think of something," said Freddy. "In fact," he added suddenly, "I *have* thought of something. Come on back out on the terrace.

Now you back me up in everything I say
—O.K.?"

"Sure, sure. Shall I giggle?"

"No, they like that. Be very solemn and serious. This'll fix 'em."

As they went back through the living room, Miss Anguish looked up. "Oh, Dr. Hopper," she tittered, "do sit down beside me and tell me all about Hollywood. I'm sure you must have had some perfectly thrilling experiences."

"I assure you, ma'am," said Freddy, "all I know about the lives of film stars is what I see on the screen. I have never been in Hollywood."

Miss Anguish drew her chin in and the corners of her mouth went down and her lower lip was pushed out, as she looked up at him with tears in her eyes. "Oh, you just *say* that!" she said with a sniffle. "I think you're mean!"

Freddy looked at Mr. Camphor, but the latter just shrugged. So Freddy shrugged back, and then he sat down beside Miss Anguish and said: "But perhaps you'd be interested in my last year's trip through the solar system." And he told her of the attempt which Mr. Bean's Uncle Ben and some of the animals had made to reach Mars, in the Benjamin Bean Space Ship. The story of this has been related elsewhere, and so I won't repeat it. Miss Anguish was thrilled by it, but when Freddy had finished, and rose and excused himself, she said: "Well, if you must go . . . But you must promise to come back later and tell me about your adventures in Hollywood."

So Freddy promised. What else could he do?

CHAPTER

5

Out on the terrace, the members of the com·
mittee were still telling jokes, and Mr. Glockenspiel was making notes of the best ones for use
in Mr. Camphor's speeches. Freddy listened for
a few minutes. He noticed that each of them
laughed harder at his own jokes than he did at

any that the others told, and nobody laughed at the jokes that Senator Blunder told except Senator Blunder. But of course, he made up for it by laughing twice as hard as anyone else. Indeed, he laughed so loud and slapped his knee and guffawed so excitedly at one of his own jokes that he ended by sticking the lighted end of his cigar back in his mouth. He jumped up and danced around, sputtering and roaring, and Mr. Slurp, thinking this was part of the joke, lay back in his chair and shouted with laughter. Of course, that made the Senator mad, and with an angry yell he went for Mr. Slurp and if the rest of the committee hadn't separated them, the results might have been serious indeed for the party.

When the excitement had died down, Mr. Slurp apologized to the Senator. "I did not realize," he said, "that my distinguished friend had burnt his tongue; I assumed that he was putting on the performance strictly for laughs. I wish to point out, however, that if performed for laughs it would be a highly entertaining caper. I would like to suggest, therefore, that—"

"I know what you're going to say," Mr. Camphor interrupted, "and I won't do it. When you're on the platform with me, if you feel that sticking the lighted end of a cigar in your mouth will get us some votes, you go ahead and do it. I won't, and that's flat."

"Gentlemen," said Freddy, "since in spite of General Wiggins's disapproval, you seem determined to continue Mr. Camphor as your candidate, there are one or two things I should like to speak about. The first is: What are the people who vote for him going to get out of electing him? I understand that the Honorable Mr. Feebler, the Democratic candidate, intends to promise that if he is elected, he will cut down taxes to half what they were last year. That's a big promise, gentlemen. Every voter in the state has to pay taxes. Unless we can promise more than that, our next governor will be the Honorable Rufus Feebler.

"Now gentlemen, Mr. Camphor has a brilliant suggestion. He suggests that we go Mr. Feebler one better. He suggests that we promise, if elected, to do away with *all* taxes! Gentlemen, on a platform like that, Mr. Camphor will sweep the state!"

The members of the committee all began talking at once. "A bold idea, Doctor," said Senator Blunder.

"But if we do away with taxes," said Mr. Glockenspiel, "who's going to pay the governor's salary?"

"And our salaries," Colonel Buglett said. "We all expect to be appointed to political jobs if Camphor is elected."

"You can't run the state government without money," said Mr. Slurp, "and the money all comes from taxes of one kind or another. I say the idea's no good."

"But don't let us be hasty," put in Judge Anguish. "The idea has merit. Unquestionably, Mr. Camphor could be elected if he promised to do away with taxes. But what then? After election, couldn't he just think things over and decide that maybe we ought to have taxes after all? The main thing is to get elected, isn't it? Probably some of the people will be mad, when their tax bill comes in. But they forget pretty quickly. No, Camphor, I think you have something there. What do you say, Buglett?"

The committee went on to discuss the proposition, and Freddy took Mr. Camphor's arm and drew him out of earshot. "Golly, Mr. Cam— I mean, Jimson, I think up the craziest things to have you do, and the crazier they are, the better they like them. Look, wouldn't it be simpler just to refuse to run?"

"I can't, Freddy. I promised. I was a fool to do it, but I won't go back on a promise. Well, you've done your best. I guess you'll just have to leave me to my fate."

"They seem determined to have you run, no matter how foolish you get," Freddy said. "Of course, you may not be elected."

"I'm afraid I will. They seem pretty sure of it this year."

"Well, let's try one more thing," said Freddy. He walked back towards the committee. "Gentlemen," he said, "we are agreed, I think, that our platform in the coming campaign is the promise to do away with all taxes. But there is another matter upon which Mr. Camphor feels very strongly—that is the question of animal suffrage. He feels that just as, years ago, women won the right to vote, today this right should be extended to animals. He feels—"

"Animals!" Senator Blunder interrupted explosively. "Did you say *animals?*"

"Animals!" said Freddy firmly. "Cows and pigs and dogs and horses—all of them are natives of our great state; they are born here, work here; they have as good a right to the vote as you or I. Remember, gentlemen, the slogan of the founders of our nation: no taxation without representation. A good slogan, but Mr. Camphor proposes a better one: no taxation, full representation. Full representation, gentlemen. Not men only. Not men and women only. Men, women, and animals—every living being that has a stake in the country should have a voice in the government, and that voice is his vote. Then this nation will be a true democracy."

"Never heard such nonsense!" Colonel Buglett growled. "You mean a mouse ought to have as much say in the government as I do?"

"A mouse," said Mr. Camphor firmly, "is smaller than Colonel Buglett. Agreed. But the right to vote is not based on size. Otherwise the vote would be restricted to cows and horses, which are larger than Colonel Buglett. Let us be consistent, gentlemen. Let us extend the vote even to guinea pigs."

"We can't support you in that kind of foolishness, Jimson," said Senator Blunder.

"If you want me to run for governor, you'll have to," Mr. Camphor replied. "For a bill to give the vote to animals is one of the first things I shall press the legislature to pass."

"My dear fellow!" Mr. Glockenspiel exclaimed. "The whole country will laugh; they'll laugh us right out of politics. Gentlemen, if Mr. Camphor is determined about this—and

I believe he is—the only thing we can do is withdraw his candidacy. Don't you agree?"

Mr. Slurp and the Senator and Colonel Buglett nodded vigorously. But Mr. Camphor, who was beginning to look much less gloomy, said: "So suppose they do laugh? That's what you wanted, wasn't it? You run me as the giggling governor—O.K., I'll make 'em giggle!"

The committee began talking together, throwing disgusted glances at Mr. Camphor, who winked delightedly at Freddy. But Judge Anguish, who had said nothing for some time, suddenly spoke. "Your proposition, Camphor," he said, "sounds pretty silly on the face of it. But you must have some good reason back of it. Do you mind telling us what it is?"

"Certainly not," Mr. Camphor replied. "The Republican party wants to win this election, doesn't it? But somewhere around half the population of the state is in New York City, and the city is Democratic. The Republicans count on the upstate vote to win, because most of upstate is Republican. But the city hasn't an awful lot of animals. Most of the animals are upstate, on farms and in the woods; and they'll vote Republican, like the farmers whose land they live on. All right—that means you can add a few million Republican votes if you grant animal suffrage. And that means a Republican administration in Albany for the next hundred years."

"H'm," said Senator Blunder, "hadn't thought of that." And the others stopped looking disgusted and began to look hopeful.

"It is truly an excellent idea," said the Judge. "Animals are certainly citizens, and as such have the right to vote. And they are good citizens; I have never heard of an animal criminal."

That was a smart idea of Mr. Camphor's, Freddy thought. But it was a smart idea in the wrong place. If he hadn't pointed out that the animal vote would make a Republican victory certain, probably they'd have refused to let him run for governor, and chosen some other candidate. Freddy frowned and shook his head at him, but Mr. Camphor was so delighted with his own idea that he forgot entirely that he was trying to get out of being elected, and when Mr. Slurp asked him how he was sure that he could get the animals to vote for him, he turned to Freddy.

"Gentlemen," he said, "my friend here, whom I have introduced as Dr. Hopper, is the answer to that question. He can deliver a state-wide animal vote to the Republican party. Why do I think he can? Because, gentlemen, he is an animal himself." And he snatched off Freddy's wig, unhooked his beard, and, with an arm across his shoulders, drew him forward. "This, my friends," he said, "is Mr. Frederick Bean, President of the First Animal Bank, Editor of the Bean Home News, head of the detective firm of Frederick & Wiggins, the most influential pig in the state. I think you have heard of him, gentlemen."

The members of the committee pressed forward to shake hands with Freddy. "A great pleasure," said Senator Blunder, "to see you again, sir." For the Senator, like all good politicians, never forgot a face, and he had once met Freddy at an evening party at Mrs. Underdunk's.

The others, of course, had heard of Freddy, and were pleased to meet him. Only Colonel Buglett seemed doubtful. "A pig?" he said. "You are a pig, are you not? Quite so. Well, if you are to take an active part in this campaign, may I suggest that you buy yourself a new outfit? That coat, those pants!" He looked Freddy up and down disgustedly.

Freddy was quite aware of the shabbiness of his costume. The coat and pants had been borrowed from a scarecrow a year earlier, and they were wrinkled and patched so that except at twilight they were scarcely correct for wear in good society. But Freddy had taken a dislike to Colonel Buglett, who from the first had seemed inclined to sneer at him.

He tipped back his head and looked down his long nose at the Colonel. "My good sir," he said snippily, "economy in government is our watchword in this campaign. And it ill befits those who go about preaching economy to wear costly raiment. The British have taken the lead in emphasizing economy and we might do well to follow them. Are you aware, sir, that at the opening of Parliament, the Marquess of Ilming, one of the richest men in England, wore a ragged shirt? And that Sir James Gobbling was out at elbows and had a hole in the seat of his pants?"

The Colonel backed down. "Er—no," he said. "Well, perhaps you're right."

Leaving the committee to discuss whether mice should be allowed to vote, or whether it should be restricted to animals twelve inches long or over, Freddy again drew Mr. Camphor aside. "Well," he said, "you fixed yourself good, Jimson. When they thought you were crazy for suggesting that animals should vote, why couldn't you leave it alone? They'd have given you the old heave ho, and you'd be out

"This, my friends, is Mr. Frederick Bean."

of politics for good. But no, you had to go point out that it would give you more votes. Why didn't you keep still?"

"I guess I *was* kind of dumb, huh?" Mr. Camphor said.

"No, you're too smart; that's worse. And you've convinced 'em that you're pretty smart, that you'd make a good governor. No use now trying to convince 'em that you aren't. I'll try to think of something else, but I don't have much hope. In the meantime, let's go have a look at Senator Blunder's room. Maybe the thief left some clue that will tell us who he was."

But though they went over the room thoroughly, they found no clues.

Freddy had put on his wig and beard again, because that was the easiest way to carry them. When they came down through the living room, Miss Anguish put down her book, which she had resumed reading, and said: "Oh, how do you do?"

Freddy thought it was a funny thing to say, when he had just left her ten minutes earlier. "Er—how do you do?" he said.

Her hands fluttered at a bow of ribbon at her throat and she looked up archly at him. "I don't think I know you, do I?" she said.

Mr. Camphor winked at the pig. "This is

Mr. Frederick Bean, the celebrated detective, Miss Anguish," he said. "I don't think you've met him."

"How do you do," said Miss Anguish. "No, I don't think so. But he does remind me so much of someone. Now who could it be?"

"Possibly old Dr. Hopper, who was here yesterday," said Mr. Camphor.

"Oh, of course!" said Miss Anguish. "Well, it's nice to see you again, Doctor. I hope your Aunt Judith is better."

"Yes," Freddy stammered. "Tha—thank you." And he bowed and hurried out. "What's the matter with her, Jimson?" he asked. "And who am I? And who's my Aunt Judith? And are you C. Jimson Camphor or General Grant?"

Mr. Camphor laughed. "She's not as queer as she sounds," he said. "Nobody's ever figured out why she does that sort of thing. Probably mixing people up is her idea of a joke."

"You were the one that was trying to mix *her* up," said Freddy. "Introducing me as two different people."

"Sure. Only you see, you can't mix her up. —Hey, look at that bird; has he got on glasses?"

"Gosh," said Freddy, "that's Uncle Solomon,

the screech owl. After me, I guess. It must be important to bring him out in the daytime. That's why he wears those dark glasses: day-light hurts his eyes."

CHAPTER

The news that Uncle Solomon had for Freddy was indeed important. Mr. Bean had been arrested. Mr. Herbert Garble's sister, Mrs. Underdunk, with whom he lived, had found a handkerchief marked W.F.B. in front of her bureau that morning, and on looking through the bureau drawers, claimed to have missed several valuable rings. She had at once called the sheriff, who had had no choice but to go out and arrest Mr. Bean and take him down to the jail.

"Why, that's outrageous!" said Freddy. "And I suppose the handkerchief was clean and unironed."

The screech owl said it was.

"H'm," said Freddy thoughtfully. "There were four handkerchiefs stolen from the Beans' clothesline, I think."

"That means that whoever stole them will probably burglarize two more houses, leaving a handkerchief in each one," said Mr. Camphor.

"Not while Mr. Bean's in jail, if they have any sense," Freddy said.

"Correct," said Uncle Solomon in his precise little voice. "That would merely be confirmation of your theory of Mr. Bean's innocence. For while in jail, Mr. Bean could certainly not be engaged in burgling, and so could not have left the third handkerchief. And if he could not have left the third handkerchief, one could assume it much less likely that he had left the first and second."

"I don't need 'em to leave any more handkerchiefs around to prove that Mr. Bean isn't a burglar," Freddy said a little crossly.

"To prove it, that's just what you do need," said the owl. "I think it is unlikely that Mr. Bean stole anything. But that is an opinion; it is not knowledge. Knowledge is something you know, and I do not *know* that he is innocent."

"Well, I do," Freddy said. "For that matter, I don't know that you're innocent either, Uncle Solomon. Maybe you stole the things. You could get in a window and steal something and leave a handkerchief."

But if Freddy hoped to make the owl mad, he failed. "Dear me," said Uncle Solomon, giving a cold little tittering laugh; "now you're beginning to think. And if you'll only think a little more along that line, you'll think of a way to get Mr. Bean out of jail."

"Golly," Freddy exclaimed after a minute. "I know what you mean. But I can't climb up into any window. Look, if I get the handkerchief for you, will you do it?"

Freddy expected that the owl would refuse, and probably laugh at him for suggesting such a dangerous mission. But for once, Uncle Solomon was serious. "You get the handkerchief," he said. "I'll do it tonight. I like your Mr. Bean," he continued. "And though you probably don't realize it, he's in a very dangerous situation."

"This handkerchief trick will get him out of it," said Freddy.

"Oh, I don't mean his being in jail. Matter of fact, he's probably safer there than he would be back in his own home."

"Good gracious," said Mr. Camphor, "you mean this revolt among the animals that Freddy has told me about? But it's silly of them to think they can take over and run things. It's—"

"Listen," the owl interrupted. "I know more about this than you suspect. I've heard a great deal, and I've put two and two together, and I do not like the answer. These talks that someone is giving up at the Grimby house—they are only part of it. They are being given for the purpose of turning farm animals against the men who own the land they live on. So that on the day when the revolution begins, there won't be much local resistance.

"But the leader of this revolution knows quite well that farm animals alone cannot seize the power. Up in the woods, across Otesaraga Lake, in the foothills of the Adirondacks, he is training an army—an army of wild animals who are no friends to humans. Animals that humans have hunted and trapped. And with them are a good many discontented farm animals. Mr. Witherspoon's horse, Jerry, is one of them. You've probably heard that he's been missing for a month. He got sick of not having enough to eat at Witherspoon's and he joined the revolutionists. And some of your Bean farm rabbits are there too.

"When the signal is given, they'll come down and drive the farmers from their farms. They're going to start right in this neighborhood around Centerboro. As soon as the farmers are driven off, they'll turn over the management of the farm to those of the farm animals who have joined up with their organization, and they'll go on to the next farm. They believe in a year, they'll have the whole state under animal control."

"My goodness," said Mr. Camphor, "that would let me out of being governor, wouldn't it?"

"It would also let you out of living on this nice estate," said the owl. "Unless you get busy, a year from now, perhaps two months, there'll be cows and horses and porcupines sitting in the comfortable chairs out there on your terrace, instead of politicians."

"Much rather have them there, too," Mr. Camphor muttered.

"But Uncle Solomon," said Freddy, "do you really think they can get away with it? Do you believe that Mr. Bean's animals will turn against him and drive him out of his home?"

"Your Mr. Bean is a special case, I admit," said the owl. "He's been nicer to his animals, and more thoughtful for their comforts, than most farmers. I think they may put up a fight for him. But suppose now that you're a pig on any of these other farms around here. You live in a dirty pig pen, and the farmer feeds you plenty, but what kind of food is it? The least you can say is that it's pretty coarse stuff, and not very daintily served either. And then somebody comes along and says: 'How'd you like to change places with this farmer, and have him live in the pen and eat out of a trough, and you sit down at the table with a nice white tablecloth with only a few spots on it, and sleep between nice clean sheets—' Well, what are you going to say to that?"

"I guess you're going to say: 'I'm for it,' " Freddy replied.

"Goodness' sake," said Mr. Camphor, "it looks as if the animals were going to get the vote whether I run for governor or not."

"Those who think they're going to have a vote under an animal dictator are very much mistaken," said Uncle Solomon. "The country will be run the way Russia is; every animal will be told what to do, and if he knows what is good for him he'll do it. Animals that try to remain loyal to their human masters will be moved out and replaced by rough characters from the Adirondacks."

Freddy said: "Jimson, I think I ought to go back to the farm and have a talk with Mrs. Wiggins and Jinx, and with Mrs. Bean, too. If you'll come with me, Uncle Solomon, we'll get that handkerchief and plan where to use it." He turned to Mr. Camphor and said: "I'm afraid I haven't been much help, but I'll come back later if you want me to. Maybe I can think of something."

"I'll drive you down," said Mr. Camphor. "And don't worry about me. After all, a governor only serves two years."

"But maybe they'll re-elect you for another term."

"You leave that to me," said Mr. Camphor with a grin.

Freddy got an unironed handkerchief marked W.F.B. from Mrs. Bean and gave it to Uncle Solomon. He and Mr. Camphor had a long talk with Mrs. Bean, and later in the afternoon he quietly notified all the animals whose loyalty he was sure of, and held a meeting in the cowbarn that evening. For the first time, Mrs. Bean was present at one of these meetings. While Freddy told of the danger that hung over the farm, and while they discussed plans for fighting off the revolutionists, she didn't say anything; but when at the end, all the animals filed past and pledged loyalty to the Bean farm, and swore to fight to the death to defend it, she cried. None of the animals had ever seen her cry before, and they were very much affected. Even Jinx, who was a pretty hard-boiled cat, was so deeply moved that for the first time in his life he made a speech.

When they had all sworn, he leaped up onto the dashboard of the old phaeton, from which the other animals who had addressed the meeting had spoken, and said: "You animals, tonight you've heard a lot of plans discussed. I've got nothing against that. You've heard a lot of patriotic talk. I've got nothing against that either. But talk is easy; talk alone ain't worth five cents a scuttleful. What we want is action. Are we just going to sit here and let these folks take our homes away from us? Or are we going to go up and take their homes away from them? Oh sure, sure—we're going to fight to the death to defend this farm. Well, why wait and let

"What we want is action!"

them bring the fight to us? Why not let them fight to the death to defend their own homes? How about it, boys; shall we sit here and wait for 'em, or who'll follow me up to their next meeting at the Grimby house tomorrow night? We'll clean up that gang, and then we'll go on up around the lake into the Adirondacks and find the rest of 'em and drive 'em back where they came from. Eh? How about it? Who's with me?"

There was a roar of applause, and a number of the more hot-headed animals crowded up towards the cat. But Mrs. Bean got to her feet; and immediately the uproar subsided.

"Animals and friends," she said, "I thank you from the bottom of my heart for this wonderful demonstration of loyalty. But I ask you to consider this: If you attempt to strike now, without organizing, without planning carefully, you may very well bring down on our heads just the fate that you are trying to escape. Before you do anything, get Mr. Bean's advice. I'm sure he'll be back home in a day or two, and then you can talk to him."

"He'll be home tomorrow," said Freddy emphatically.

"I hope you're right," Mrs. Bean said. "Goodness, I just baked him an apple pie, and it makes me want to cry every time I look at it and think of him sitting down in that old jail, gnawing at a dry crust—"

"The sheriff sets a good table, ma'am," said Freddy. "He's probably gnawing at roast turkey and plum pudding. But I'll take that pie down to him if you say so."

"Why, thank you, Freddy. That would be real nice. But what I was saying," she went on: "Talk to Mr. Bean before you do anything. If more people would talk to Mr. Bean before they do things, there'd be less trouble in the world."

CHAPTER

7

The following morning Freddy and Jinx took the apple pie down to Mr. Bean in the Centerboro jail. It was a fine day and the prisoners were all sitting out on the lawn under striped umbrellas, reading and talking and playing games. Mr. Bean was playing croquet with the sheriff, who promptly invited the two animals to stay to lunch.

When they were away from the barnyard, Mr. Bean didn't seem to mind so much hearing animals talk, and he discussed things very freely with Jinx and Freddy. "You tell Mrs. B. not to worry about me," he said. "This is a real nice jail, and to tell you the truth, I've been thinking she might like it here herself. Maybe she'd like to commit a small crime of some kind, and come down for a week or two. Make a nice change for her. There's lots to do, and good food and good company, and you animals can run the farm all right." He fizzed with laughter behind his whiskers. Evidently he wasn't much worried about the burglary charge.

But he was very much disturbed about what they had to tell him concerning the revolt among the animals. "As you know, Freddy," he said, "I ain't one to interfere in animal affairs. I let you handle things in your own way. But in this, I guess we'll have to work together. Fight together too, maybe. But we'll talk about that later. There goes the dinner bell."

Jinx and Freddy had lunch at the sheriff's table, along with Mr. Bean and a burglar named Bloody Mike. Mike had won his nickname not because he was a specially ferocious fighter, but because whatever he did, he was always bumping his head or cutting his finger or walking into the edge of an open door. When he went out to burgle a house, he invariably came back covered with scratches and bruises, and he said himself that he couldn't pare an apple without cutting his finger half off. But he was very good company, and that was why he was invited to sit at the sheriff's table.

So they had a pleasant lunch, and for dessert they had the apple pie. Mike, whose table manners weren't very good, even for a burglar, picked up his piece and started to bite the end off. And then he said: "Ouch!" in a loud voice, and dropped the pie on his plate and put his hand up to his jaw.

"It would be me that bit on that rock," he said.

"A rock?" Mr. Bean exclaimed. "In one of Mrs. Bean's pies? Well, she *must* have been upset! Gracious, Mike, I'm awful sorry. Did you bust the tooth?"

"Just kinda sprained it, like," said the burglar. "Think nothing of it, William. Hey, it ain't a rock either." He poked in the pie with his fork, and presently drew out a file. "Oho," he said, "seems like your wife thinks you don't like it here!"

"Good grief!" said Mr. Bean. "Sheriff, on behalf of Mrs. Bean, I want to apologize to you. Guess she's forgotten what a nice jail you run. If I've told her once, I've told her forty times how the iron bars on your windows work."

Some years earlier, the prisoners had complained about the bars on their windows—said they made them feel shut in. So the sheriff had them just set in frames that could be swung out like windows. So that while to the citizens of Centerboro, they looked like good strong prison windows, if the prisoner inside wanted to escape, all he had to do was swing the framework out and jump to the ground. As a matter of fact no prisoner ever bothered to do this, because if he wanted to go out he just said to the sheriff: "Think I'll go down to the movies," or "Guess I'll go see my aunt," and then walked out the front door. But he had to be back by eleven o'clock.

The sheriff poked gingerly at his piece of pie. "Just want to be sure there ain't a couple of machine guns in here," he said. "Does your wife always put such strong seasoning in your pies?"

Later in the afternoon they were playing Prisoners' Base on the lawn with the other prisoners, when the sheriff was called to the door. When he came back, he said: "Well, William, Hank's here for you with the buggy. Judge Willey has just signed an order for your release. It seems that there was a burglary at Dr. Wintersip's last night, and one of your handkerchiefs was found on the floor. Of course you were in jail, so you couldn't have been the burglar, and that makes it look as if you were innocent of the other two burglaries. Congratulations. Not that I ever thought you'd gone in for burglary at your age," he added.

Mike said he sometimes wished he had never taken up burglary professionally. "There ain't really any future in it," he said.

"Yeah?" said a prisoner named Louie the Lump, "that ain't very complimentary to the sheriff, here. You made out all right, Mike, didn't you—landing in a nice jail like this? What more future do you want?"

"Well," Mike said, "what I want is just what I got—a nice place to live and good company. But it ain't burglary. A good burglar thinks it's a disgrace to get caught and jailed. Me, I get out, and I just live for the time when I stand up before the judge and he says: 'Six months in the county jail.' "

"I don't blame you," Mr. Bean said. "If I wasn't married and didn't have a farm to look after, I'd commit a real bang-up good crime and try to get sent up here for life. As it is, I guess I'd better get back home." So he said good-by and got in the buggy and drove Freddy and Jinx home.

They had almost reached the farm when Mr. Bean pulled up suddenly. He pointed to a poster on a tree by the roadside. "That isn't a regular 'no trespassing' notice," he said. "Go get it, Freddy."

So Freddy hopped down and ripped the poster from the tree and brought it back.

They looked at it in silence. There was a picture of a man with a gun standing beside a bear he had shot. Above in large print, it said: "Will You Be Next?" And underneath: "How long does it take you, animals, to learn that men are your deadly enemies? How long will you submit to be beaten and starved and shot by them? Now is your chance—the first real chance in a thousand years—to get back the right to live as free animals in a world that belongs to you, not to your so-called masters. Join up today." And the poster was signed with a large S.

"You know who S is?" Mr. Bean demanded.

The animals shook their heads.

"Well, if he ain't a man, he's got a man helping him. Because this here poster was printed in a print shop, and no animal could do that. Hey, Hank; turn around. We'll go see Mr. Dimsey."

Mr. Dimsey was the publisher of the Centerboro *Guardian* and he also printed Freddy's newspaper, the *Bean Home News*. When he was shown the poster, he frowned. "No, I didn't print that," he said, "but it was printed here on my press—I recognize the type. And I know when it was printed. I was home with the flu for ten days a week or so ago, and when I came back to the shop I saw somebody had been here, working with the press. Nothing was taken, and everything was in order, so I didn't make a fuss about it."

"You know who it was?" Freddy asked.

"I've got a pretty good idea. Herb Garble had the *Guardian* once; he can set type and run a press. Far as I know, he's the only other printer in town."

They thanked him and went on home. They saw more posters on the way, and each time Freddy climbed out and tore them down.

Freddy found that there had been developments while he was away. Mrs. Wiggins said that she was followed wherever she went by spies—rabbits, usually; and several of the other animals said they had the impression that they were being watched, but they couldn't pin the impression down definitely. Mr. Pomeroy reported that Mr. Garble had been seen up by the Grimby house several times, but since he owned the Big Woods, there was nothing really very peculiar about that. The robin also reported that some bumblebees, who had flown up across Otesaraga Lake and cruised along the edge of the Adirondacks, had brought word of a good deal of activity in the forest. They had seen a lot of cows and horses, who don't usually live in the woods; as well as a number of big shaggy dogs, such as they had never seen before. The posters showing the man with the bear he had shot, as well as others showing animals in cages, or tied up, or with muzzles on, had been tacked up all around the Centerboro region. What was even more serious, a good many farm animals had already left their homes and apparently joined up with the rebels.

That was the last peaceful day that the Bean farm was to enjoy for many weeks. Early in the afternoon Uncle Solomon flew down to see

Freddy. With him was Old Whibley. It was unusual for the screech owl to come out in the daytime; it was unheard of for Whibley. They had come to warn the Beans. The woods up north of the lake were fairly boiling with animals—tough old horses and cattle from northern hill farms, bears and bobcats and coyotes and even a few panthers. "Hasn't been a panther in the state before in seventy-five years," said Whibley.

"What do you think we ought to do?" Freddy asked.

"Get out!" said Old Whibley explosively. "Get away while you can, and take the Beans with you."

"But why?" said Freddy. "After all, what can they do? And these little meetings at the Grimby house—"

"These little meetings, as you call them," said Uncle Solomon, "are one small part of a big scheme. The speaker gets the farm animals discontented with their life, he tells them that they are fools to let humans rule them. He tells them lies about humans, and because he repeats his lies, they believe them. He's a rabble rouser, and a good one."

"I suppose you mean by that," Freddy said, "that he is a clever speaker who can stir up his

Mrs. Wiggins said she was followed by spies.

listeners to any crazy kind of violent action that he tells them to take. Yes, I heard him; it's true. But he didn't stir up me or Jinx, or you, Uncle Solomon."

"We are loyal, and we've got some sense—at least I have," said the screech owl with his tittering laugh. "I'm sometimes not so sure about you. Not when you talk as if whoever it is that makes those speeches up at the Grimby house is just a joke."

"Do you know who he is?" Freddy asked.

Both owls shook their heads. "We've never seen him. But whoever he is, he must come from this neighborhood, to know as much as he does about all these farmers. And he's not a man; no man could move around among those burned beams in the Grimby cellar—he'd be too big."

"But his voice," said Freddy. "It's—goodness, it's big. Bigger than any man's."

"So was the voice of that clockwork boy Mr. Benjamin Bean built," said Whibley.

"Golly, that's right," said the pig. "He had a microphone built in him, and that rooster, Ronald, used to run him. Why, if he turned the sound up, a mouse could be heard all over the farm. But you don't think it's a little animal that's making those speeches, do you?"

"Don't you read your history?" said Uncle Solomon. "Hitler was an insignificant-looking little man, but he was one of the greatest rabble rousers that ever lived."

"Oh dear," said Freddy, "you really think we're in danger? What could those animals do? Mr. Bean has a gun, and he could telephone the sheriff, if any animals came around and started to destroy things."

"We can't do more than warn you," said Old Whibley. "It's our belief that that mob up in the woods is about ready to march. If they do, Mr. Bean's gun will be about as much protection as a cap pistol. Well, we've said our say. Come along, Sol." And he spread his big wings and flew off.

Uncle Solomon started to follow, then paused. "You have disappointed me, pig," he said. "I assured Whibley that you would take our advice. But I see that the natural stupidity of the porcine race has finally extinguished the feeble glimmers of intelligence which I have sometimes thought to discern in you. A pity." His cold little laugh rippled out and then he too went.

CHAPTER

8

Freddy's effort to persuade Mr. Bean to abandon the farm was, as he had expected, useless. Mr. Bean flatly refused. "I ain't going to run from an enemy I haven't seen," he said. "Oh, I know that these animals could make a lot of trouble, but if we stick together we can fight 'em off."

There seemed to be nothing to do but wait, so Freddy decided to go and see if he could persuade Mr. Camphor to come down and stay at the Beans' where at least they would all be together. He went up through the Big Woods, giving the Grimby house a wide berth, then across a corner of the Schermerhorn farm and along the edge of the Witherspoon pastures to the top of the hill, from which he could see the blue waters of the lake. Beside the lake, surrounded by green lawns, stood the Camphor mansion.

Freddy was nearly a mile away, but he was remarkably far-sighted, and on the terrace before the house, he could see the committee sitting in their garden chairs. But what made him stop and stare—on the lawn that sloped down from the terrace to the lake four bark canoes were pulled up. And around them were grouped a number of men on whose oiled bodies the sun glinted. He could even make out that several of the men had their heads shaved, except for the long scalp lock. Indians! Well, he knew that there were some Indians living in the woods; they made things—moccasins and baskets of sweet grass and such, that they sold to summer people. But they were tame Indians, civilized Indians. And this looked like a war party.

"Golly," he said to himself, "I wonder if I ought to go down! I don't want to get massacred." But the committee seemed to be taking it calmly. It looked pretty safe. So he went on.

Miss Anguish had joined the committee on the terrace, and she waved to Freddy and patted the seat of a chair beside her. "Sit here, Chief," she said. "Unless you're taking part in the dance."

Mr. Camphor said: "This is Frederick Bean, the poet, Miss Anguish. You met him yesterday. The chief is the one with the feather headdress, just getting his make-up on."

"But that's black and white he's putting on— war paint!" Freddy exclaimed. "Is this business safe?"

"Sure. I've known these Indians a long time. They're Otesaragas—I think some offshoot of the Six Nations. They have a settlement about thirty miles north of the lake, and summers they come down and sell stuff to tourists and summer people. I asked them to come down and put on a dance for the committee."

Miss Anguish put fluttering fingers on Freddy's arm. "Tell me, Chief, have you lifted any good scalps lately?" she asked, and gave a trill of silver laughter that reminded him of Uncle Solomon.

Freddy said: "Haven't had much luck lately. But—" he lowered his voice, "we've got a nice raid coming up. We're planning to raid the Centerboro Rotary Club meeting tomorrow night. The trouble is, so many of the members are bald. Not much good as decorations."

"You ought to raid it on Ladies' Night," said Miss Anguish, and laughed again. "Look, they're going to dance; aren't you going to join them?"

Freddy grinned. "I think I'll sit this one out," he said. "Hey, what's Jimson doing?"

Mr. Camphor, who had been talking with the chief, had suddenly stripped off his coat and shirt and the chief was painting his face and chest in broad bars of black and white. "For goodness' sake, is he going on the war path?"

Mr. Camphor swam a good deal during the summer; his skin was sunburned nearly as dark as the Indians'. Now when with a tomahawk in his hand he took his place among the others who began yelling and stamping and cavorting in a circle on the grass, Freddy had a hard time distinguishing him from the Indians. "Gosh, they look just like the Horribles!" Freddy thought, remembering the way the disguised rabbits had pranced and flourished knives about their scared victims.

"Very pretty dance," said Miss Anguish. "So dignified and graceful." Freddy glanced at her, but she seemed to be quite serious. He wondered how she could always manage to make her remarks have so little reference to what she talked about.

The dance went on for some time. Most of the Indians wore khaki pants and moccasins, and only two had their heads shaved except for the scalp lock; the others wore their black hair like white men, only rather longer.

The committee paid little attention to the war dance. They were still busy digging into their memories for old jokes for Mr. Camphor to tell on the platform. They had decided that he should give each of them credit for his own jokes; as for instance—"This reminds me of a favorite story of Senator Blunder's," and then he would tell the joke. They liked this idea, because each was sure that his own jokes were the funniest, and each expected to get a good deal of credit from Mr. Camphor's tell-

Now with a tomahawk he took his place.

ing them. After all, what better reason is there for voting for a congressman than that he's made you laugh?

After the dance was over, the chief came up and was thanked and congratulated by the committee members. He smiled and grunted, and then turned back to the canoes. Presently they pushed off. It wasn't until they were well out on the lake that Freddy noticed that the bowman in the first canoe had sandy hair. And then he looked around and didn't see Mr. Camphor anywhere.

Miss Anguish noticed that he was disturbed. She gave him a surprisingly shrewd glance. "I think they kidnapped the Governor," she said.

It seemed so unlikely that anything Miss Anguish said could have the faintest relation to the facts, that Freddy hesitated. Then without saying anything, he got up and went into the house to find Bannister.

The butler, after a short search, said that Mr. Camphor wasn't in the house. "But I wouldn't worry, sir. They made him a member of the tribe last summer. Quite a gay ceremony, sir. They also honored me in the same way. We are both members of the Beaver Clan of the Otesaraga tribe. I could have joined the dance, but there is so little dignity here today . . . ," he glanced out of the window towards the snickering committee, "that I thought, better not."

"Well, I don't like it," Freddy said. "He certainly wouldn't go off with the Indians willingly."

"I think, sir, that's just what he did do," said Bannister. "I fancy he feels that the only way he can get out of being governor is to take to the woods."

"Well, it's a poor place to take to right now," said Freddy. And he told Bannister about the animals who were gathering there for the attack on the farms.

" 'Pon my word, sir," Bannister said, "that is indeed serious. What do you suggest that we do?"

"Get out those camping things we used when we went camping across the lake two years ago. We'll have to go after him."

"Splendid, sir!" Bannister exclaimed. "As an adopted Otesaraga brave, I can take you straight to the Indian village. It'll be very jolly to get into the woods again. All this dignity, it gets on one's nerves a bit after a time, sir. But it is late, wouldn't it be better to start in the morning? And what shall we tell the committee?"

"I guess the easiest thing is to tell them that he's been kidnapped by the Indians, and we're going to rescue him. Now I'll have to go back to the farm. I'll be back first thing in the morning."

"I'll have everything ready, sir," said the butler. "Won't you take the car? I'm sure Mr. Camphor would want you to."

"Maybe he would, since he's never seen me drive," said Freddy with a grin.

Freddy had his own plane and was an expert flier, but he was not a good car driver. He explained this by saying that while up in the air, you had plenty of room; on the ground, there were too many things around: trees and telegraph posts and other cars and dogs and cats. He never hit things very hard, but he hit them often. Fortunately, he had no car of his own, and the first time he borrowed a car from one of his Centerboro friends was usually also the last.

Now as he drove out of the gate, he heard a click as the bumper nicked the gatepost. "Confound it," he said, "I gave that thing plenty of room. It just deliberately moved closer when I went through." He drove more carefully after that. But as he turned into the Centerboro road, he narrowly missed a cat, who leaped aside with a screech.

"Darn you, cat," he shouted, "why don't you —Oh, it's you, Jinx," he said, recognizing his friend.

"Wouldn't have been me if I hadn't been darn quick on my feet," said the cat. "I came to look for you, Freddy." He hopped into the car. "Here's news for you. I got a new title. I'm General Jinx, new head of the Bean farm. Henceforth and hereafter you don't take orders from Mr. Bean, you take 'em from me."

Freddy wrinkled up his nose. "What are you talking about? You got delusions of grandeur or something?"

"You bet I got something. Listen, kid. Just after you left a couple of J.J.'s spies brought word that old Garble was up at the Grimby house. So I went up and sure enough, there he was squatting on the edge of the cellar hole and talking to somebody down inside. I snuck up as close as I could but I couldn't hear what they said. But at last Garble gets up and beats it. So I figure: What the heck, it can't be any very big animal down in that mess of tangled up beams and stuff, so very carefully I tiptoed down the cellar stairs and crawled through and over and under until I got to the bottom. Then I stayed perfectly still for ten minutes. And what do you think came out? I'll give you ten guesses.''

"I can't think of any animal that would stay in a place like that except a rat," Freddy said, "and the rats are all in Montana—all except Eli. But Eli was never a leader, he just obeyed Simon's orders. This animal, whoever he is, is a bold and dangerous character.''

"That's fairly good guessing," said Jinx. "Well, I'll tell you a little more. There was a sort of box on the cellar floor, with what looked like a microphone attached to it. I'm certain it's the one Uncle Ben rigged up in the clockwork boy. And then as I watched, an animal came out and began fooling with it. He was pretty near as big as I am, and he was gray, with a sharp nose and a long scaly tail—''

"Not Simon!" Freddy exclaimed.

"Yeah. It was the old wretch himself. Back from the wide-open spaces where rats are rats and men tip their hats to them. Yeah, he told me later that Garble sent for him and his family and paid the express. But I just watched, and then I pounced and got him. Golly, how he squealed when I tickled him—you know how he hates to be tickled. He spilled the whole thing —this revolution idea was Garble's, and the rats hate us and the Beans; they were only too willing to take over the farm.

"But listen—this is the pay-off. Finally, when I'd got it all out of him, I said: 'Well, I guess this puts the lid on your revolution. This time we'll ship you off to South America, and let's see Garble get you back from there.' So then he wanted to make a dicker with me. If I'd let him go, when the revolution got going he'd have me put in charge of the Bean farm. Boy, what a picture he painted! Me, sleeping every night on the guest-room bed, and Mrs. Bean cooking up fancy food for me, and a quart of cream every meal. I didn't tell him I couldn't have all that cream, that I had to watch my figure.

"Or I could order the Beans into exile—off in Canada somewhere—and get some other humans to work for me. He sure almost had me sold on it.

"Oh no, he didn't really. But I got to thinking. I had Simon, but I didn't have Garble, and even if we got rid of Simon, Garble could put Ezra or Zeke in his place, and the revolution would go on just the same. So I said to myself: Suppose I accept. I'll be on the inside and know everything they're up to. I can work with the A.B.I. and maybe I can blow their plans

sky-high. Eh? How about it? Jinx, the old su-
per-spy, hey? Jinx Tracy to the rescue!"

Freddy said it was a good idea. "But it's dangerous. If they find out—"

"Who's going to tell 'em? Nobody'll know
but you and J.J., and my contact—probably that
bumblebee, Horace. There's a meeting tonight
again at the Grimby house. I said I'd speak. You
better come—boy, am I going to blast your
character!" He giggled. "You don't merely steal
candy from kids, you steal worms from robins!"
He paused. "Well, what do you think?" he
asked seriously.

"It's dangerous," Freddy replied. "But if
you're willing to do it—well, Mr. and Mrs.
Bean and every animal on the farm will be
grateful. But they won't be grateful until after
it's all over and Simon and Garble are in jail.
Because you mustn't let anybody but me know
what you're up to. Mr. and Mrs. Bean and
all your friends must think you've sold them
out, that you're a traitor. Your good name will
be gone. Why, the name of Jinx will be dragged
in the gutter. Good gracious, it will be just soz-
zled up and down in the mud."

"I know." For the first time since Freddy had
known him, Jinx looked worried. "But what
else can I do? Suppose Simon and these other

animals do take over the farm. I could make things a lot easier for my friends—even for the Beans, maybe. No, I've got to do it, Freddy. I owe a lot to the Beans." He grinned. "Sound pretty noble, don't I? But I mean it. So let's go have a talk with J.J."

CHAPTER

9

That night Freddy disguised himself and went up to the Grimby house again. There was a mob of animals there, and Freddy couldn't get very close to the cellar, partly because there seemed to be a bodyguard of big shaggy dogs protecting the speakers. First, Simon spoke, urging his hearers to join up at once. "The hour of action draws near," he said. "Do not delay. Soon we will march—and remember, my friends, when we do, those who are not with us are against us. Those who hope to stand idly by and watch to see which side wins—all those will be considered our enemies.

"Join us now, or be crushed by us later. You have only a little time—a matter of hours. Delay means exile, or prison—or worse. I repeat—join us now, or be crushed by us later!

"And now, my friends, I have a wonderful surprise for you. One of the staunchest defenders of the Bean farm, one of the oldest and most important of that group of barnyard animals who have for so long been trusted retainers of the house of Bean, has come over to our side. Friends, I present to you the new captain and leader of the Bean farm—that fierce fighter and distinguished statesman—Jinx!"

There was a buzz of excitement among the audience, and some scattered cheering. But the little voice, that had spoken up for Mr. Bean at the previous meeting, cut through the noise. "Traitor!" it squeaked.

There was a flurry of activity down by the cellar steps and a squeal of pain, and then Jinx's voice said: "No, let him go. Don't hit him. We can appreciate courage, my friends, and we can honor it, even in an enemy."

A rabbit bounded off away from the cellar, and then Jinx spoke again. "My friends, I have always had at heart the best interests of animals, and particularly of the animals of the Bean farm. In opposing my old comrades, in taking sides against them, I feel that I am acting in their best interests. If this is treachery—then I am indeed a traitor. If it is treachery to prevent them from destroying themselves out of a false loyalty to an unjust master, then I am indeed a traitor. If . . ."

He went on for some time explaining how noble he was. It was really quite a good speech, considering that he didn't mean a word of it.

Freddy slipped away after a while. Crossing the back road, which divided the Big Woods from the Bean woods, he saw headlights approaching, and ducked back among the trees. When the car was almost abreast of Freddy, a big gray dog jumped out into the road and stood there, in the full glare of the headlights. The driver jammed on the brakes. "Get out of the way, you fool dog," he shouted, and blew his horn. Freddy recognized Mr. Schermerhorn's voice.

But the dog didn't move. He lifted up his muzzle and gave a queer sort of howl, and there was a rustling and trampling in the bushes and three cows came out into the road. They were rawboned, rangy creatures, with long horns. One of them said: "Get out of the car, bud, if you don't want to get hurt." And then all three hooked their horns under the car body and with a heave overturned it. Mr. Schermerhorn leaped out and ran off yelling.

The cows broke into rough laughter. "I could 'a' hooked him and given him something to holler for," said one.

"No rough stuff," said the dog. "Orders are, if they don't resist, don't hurt 'em."

Freddy tiptoed away. He shivered slightly. That big gray dog with the slanting eyes— wasn't he a wolf? And if there were wolves in the Big Woods . . .

He hurried back to the farm and reached the barnyard just as Jinx was coming home. "Been up to the Grimby house?" the cat asked. "Quite a meeting, hey? How'd you like my big treachery speech?"

"You know about the wolves?" Freddy asked.

"Yeah." Jinx looked serious. "I found out Simon got a bunch of 'em down from the North on a promise of free chickens. That means we'll have to move Charles and his family. How about up in the loft over the stable? There'll be some raids from now on."

"I saw one tonight," said Freddy, and told about the overturning of Mr. Schermerhorn's car. "But there's more trouble up at Camphor's," he went on. "I'm afraid Mr. Camphor's in danger." And when he had finished his story: "Darn it, Jinx," he said, "how can I go after Mr. Camphor when there's so much danger of trouble here at the farm? I ought to be here."

"Yeah?" said the cat. "What can you do against a gang of wolves? Look, Freddy; from what I've heard, we've got about three days. There'll be some raiding first, then in two or three days the big attack. As far as the farm goes, I can handle it for that time. Even after the farm's taken over—and don't kid yourself, it *will* be taken over—I can keep the Beans from getting hurt or being thrown out. I'm really in charge there—until they find me out. Shucks, I had a talk with Garble tonight. Boy, is he rabid against you! Know what I told him?" The cat grinned. "I said you were just the front in the detective business, the big mouth. I said Wiggins solved all your cases. And I said I

wrote all your poetry. Yeah, and I said—"
Jinx stopped. "No, I better not tell you that;
you might get mad. Not that I'd blame you," he
added with a chuckle.

Freddy knew that the cat wanted him to try
to find out what scandalous thing he had said,
so he changed the subject. "You're sure it'll be
two or three days before there's any trouble
here?"

"Any big trouble—yes. You can go after
Mr. Camphor, get him, and bring him with you.
You'll be north of the lake. That's where all
those wild animals and the gangs from the hill
farms are waiting."

"And the wolves," said Freddy with a shud-
der.

"Wolves won't bother campers. They've had
strict orders to wait for the signal, and the signal won't be given for several days. Just be disguised, that's all. Don't let 'em know you're a
pig. Boy, I don't suppose some of those big
brutes have ever had even a nibble at a nice fat
pig." He smacked his lips. "Makes me kind of
envious of them, when they do catch up with
you."

This line of talk didn't seem very funny to
Freddy, and he said so. Jinx at once became serious and assured him again that there would

be no danger. "Garble wants to make the change over from men to animals without any rough stuff, if he can. Even if they found you out, I don't think they'd eat you. But they'd probably turn you over to Garble. So keep that long nose of yours covered."

Freddy didn't sleep well that night. Giant wolves with the heads of alligators were snuffling on his trail as he ran desperately down endless forest paths. When they caught him, he woke up, and he woke a dozen times during the night. He was pretty tired by morning. But he was up early, and by seven o'clock had breakfasted and told Mrs. Bean where he was going, and was on his way.

The committee were still in their beds when Freddy and Bannister pushed off in their heavily loaded canoe. Freddy wore the bright checked shirt and the coonskin cap that he had worn on their previous camping trip, but Bannister was still in his butler's getup of starched shirt and tailcoat. The only concession he made to forest travel was to exchange his black shoes for a pair of moccasins.

They paddled straight across the lake to Lakeside, the summer hotel run by Mr. Camphor's friend, Mrs. Filmore. From there, the trail went north to the Indian village. But the

They paddled straight across the lake.

Indians had not taken the trail. They had camped on the shore below the hotel, and when Freddy and Bannister climbed out of their canoe, the men of the tribe were sitting on the dock smoking, while the women, whom Freddy had not seen before, were up on the broad porch, spreading out the contents of their packs —hunting shirts and beaded moccasins and sweet-grass baskets—for sale to the guests, who were crowding round them.

Bannister went up to the chief and raised his right hand. "How," he said.

"How," the chief replied.

They talked together for a few minutes in what Freddy supposed was the Otesaraga language, then Bannister said: "The chief says Mr. Camphor has gone fishing with Running Deer. He'll be back after a while. He says Mr. Camphor ran away because he didn't want to be governor."

"That's what I thought," Freddy said. "But he'll have to come home. It's too dangerous in the woods. You ought to tell the chief, it may be dangerous for the Indians too. Though maybe the animals won't bother them."

"I told him that. He says Mr. Camphor will be all right with the Indians. They're going to go farther north and east for the rest of the summer, until the wolves are out of the woods."

"Wolf no bad," said the chief. "But cow in woods, ugh, heap bad medicine!"

"Oh," said Freddy, "I didn't know you talked English."

"Sure," said the chief. "Talk-um good. Pale-face talk. Ugh."

"You talk-um fine," said Freddy.

"Sure," said the chief. "Grass-on-face, he safe with Injun. Wolf no bite-um, cow no hook-um. He stay with Injun."

"Grass-on-face is Mr. Camphor's Indian name," Bannister explained. "His mustache, I fancy."

"You like buy-um deerskin shirt?" the chief asked. "My squaw she make-um, she sell-um. She come now." He nodded towards a fat Indian woman, with her black hair hanging in two braids beside her face, who came towards them holding out a fringed buckskin shirt. Freddy felt of it. It was as soft as silk. He wanted it. He thought it would go nicely with the coon-skin hat.

He said: "Me like-um shirt. How much?"

"Fi'teen dolla'," said the squaw. "Look nice with cap." She held it up against him. "Wah!"

she exclaimed. "White brother look like Davy Crockett."

Freddy said: "I like. I like buy. But—" He slapped his pocket—"me no got much wampum."

The chief and his wife looked at each other and burst out laughing. "Wampum!" said the chief. "I'll bet it's ten years since I've heard that word." He was speaking perfectly good English. "We must remember to use it on the customers, Ella."

Freddy was taken aback. "Hey," he said, "what's the idea of making me talk that Injun Joe talk. You speak better English than I do." He turned to Bannister. "I feel silly," he said.

"No need to," said the squaw. "We just use that kind of talk on the customers. Summer people seem to expect it. Henry and I have both been through high school, but do you think people would buy baskets and stuff from us if we talked good English?"

"If you really want that shirt," said the chief, "we'll trust you. You're a friend of Mr. Camphor's. Old Grass-on-face," he added with a grin, then turned, and said something in Otesaraga to Bannister.

The butler laughed. "He says your name in Indian is Ham-that-walks."

"You mean you knew I was a pig? In this getup? But how . . ."

"We're Indians," the chief replied. "We're trained to notice little things that a white man would miss. Like how long your nose is and you haven't any eyebrows, and your feet don't fit those moccasins. Anyway, we've heard of you from Mr. Camphor. He said you'd probably come after him."

The sputter of a gasoline engine which had been audible for some time now grew louder, and an open launch, slowly towing a small houseboat, headed for the hotel dock. Freddy recognized it as the houseboat on which he had spent a summer several years ago as Mr. Camphor's caretaker. On the upper deck, still sitting in wicker chairs and roaring with laughter, were the committee. Evidently the supply of jokes had not yet been exhausted.

Just as the houseboat was tying up at the dock, a canoe came around the point and slid up to the pilings. In it were an Indian and Mr. Camphor and a string of fish. But Mr. Camphor was not easy to recognize. He had shaved off his mustache and painted his face in bars of yellow and black. He climbed out of the canoe and walked up to the houseboat, holding up his catch. "You buy-um fish?" he said to Senator

Blunder, who with the rest of the committee was leaning over the rail, looking down at him.

"No, no," said the Senator, shaking his head. "We no buy-um fish. We look for Mr. Camphor. Man live over there." He pointed across the lake.

"You look for Mis'er Camphum—big fat man. Sure, we know."

"No, he's not fat," said Colonel Buglett. "He little, insignificant-looking feller. Bristly mustache. You know um? You see um today?"

"Oh, insignifcum, hey?" returned Mr. Camphor. "You call him name. Me no like. Me his friend. Me come when sun gone down. Kerow!" He made a circular movement with one finger over the top of his head. "Take scalp. Camphum hang 'em in tepee."

"Isn't there anybody here that speaks English?" Judge Anguish demanded. "Oh, here you, Bannister. I didn't see you. What are you doing over here?"

"The same thing you are, sir," said the butler. "Looking for Mr. Camphor. Mr. Frederick and I rather thought the Indians might have kidnapped him. But as you see, sir, he's not with them."

"On the other hand," Freddy put in hastily,

"if they intend to scalp him or burn him at the stake or something like that, they might have sent him on to the village under guard. I notice that two Indians are missing."

"Good gracious," said the judge, "you mean they really go in for that sort of thing nowadays —burning and scalping?"

"Oh, I think only once in a while. They will have their fun, you know."

"Fun!" the judge exclaimed. "Really, Mr., —ah, Freddy!"

"I'm only quoting them, sir," said the pig.

"But shouldn't we go after them—rescue him?" said Mr. Glockenspiel. "At least—well, we could call the state troopers."

"That would only seal his fate, I'm afraid. The troopers would find no sign of him at the village. And—well, sir, it wouldn't be too healthy for you if you did call the troopers. The Indians are very revengeful. They might even vote Democratic."

The committee looked alarmed. They discussed the matter for a few minutes among themselves. Presently Colonel Buglett summed up the general feeling. "Well," he said, "I do not propose to risk *my* life to rescue Camphor, if the Indians really have got him. All we know for sure is that he has disappeared. I suggest that we go back to his house and await his return. There is no need of questioning the Indians and arousing their enmity."

"If you will permit me to say so," Freddy said, "I think that is the wisest course. If he does not return after say a week—well, the state will have lost a fine governor. But I beg you, don't attempt to prove anything against the Indians if he doesn't show up. Eh, Grass-on-face?" he said, turning to Mr. Camphor. "You no like-um police, eh? Somebody send police after you, you heap mad, eh?"

"Me kill-um." Mr. Camphor made a ferocious face. "Me scalp-um." Then he drew himself up and began to make an oration in Otesaragan, or what sounded like it. It was a long oration.

Freddy pretended to translate, although he had not understood a word, and he doubted if Mr. Camphor had either. "He warns you," Freddy said, "not to interfere in the affairs of the tribe. He says that if you do, the tribe will hunt you down, burn your wigwams—by which I suppose he means your houses—and take your scalps and those of your families to decorate their lodges. And I really think, gentlemen, that he means it. I strongly advise that you go back and wait."

"Is that all he said?" asked Colonel Buglett. "Why, he talked for ten minutes."

"I didn't translate it all," Freddy said. "He was describing just what he and his friends would do to you, and somehow—well, I didn't think you'd care to hear it."

The committee didn't hang around after that. Mr. Slurp started the engine of the launch. As the houseboat drew away from the dock, Mr. Camphor turned to Freddy. "I make-um fine speech. Ugh."

"I make-um darn good translation, and a couple of ughs," Freddy replied. "Now you just stay away for a week and they'll go on home and elect somebody else."

CHAPTER

10

Freddy tried to persuade Mr. Camphor to get out of the woods. "At least, if you want to duck the committee, come stay at the farm. Or in Centerboro," he said.

But Mr. Camphor said he was going to stay with the Indians for a while. "They know how to protect themselves from wolves," he said. "And as far as danger goes, from what you tell me, there'll be more danger at the farm than in the Indian village. You'd better stay here with me, Freddy. This business may be dangerous for animals, but I can't believe it will be for humans."

Freddy thought he ought to get back to the farm, but he finally agreed to camp out two days, at Jones's Bay, where they had camped a couple of summers earlier. The Indians agreed to camp with them, and to accompany Mr. Camphor back to the village.

Horace was a bumblebee; he was attached to the A.B.I. and was one of Mr. Pomeroy's ablest investigators. At five the next morning, Horace started out in a beeline—which is what nearly all bees travel in of course—for Mr. Camphor's house. Arrived there, he went buzzing around the house, investigating the open bedroom windows. He heard a variety of snores from the various committee members, but he found neither Freddy nor Bannister nor Mr. Camphor in any of the beds.

A less experienced operative might at this point have given up. But Horace had seen a family of swallows perched on the electric-light wire, waiting for some breakfast to fly by, and he went and questioned them. He felt safe in doing this, for very few swallows will try to eat a bumblebee; which is not only a pretty large mouthful, but also has a businesslike sting. He learned about the camping party, and at once set out—in a beeline again—across the lake.

Freddy and Bannister were sleeping on their backs in the little tent, with their feet sticking out into the early morning sunlight. They appeared to be having a snoring contest. Horace, who in his investigation of the Camphor house, had been much impressed by the volume of sound produced by Senator Blunder, was particularly envious of Freddy's snore, which was rather musical. There were none of the gasps and whistles and sudden ferocious snorts which the committee had been producing, but a sort of deep buzzing, rather like a giant bumblebee practicing the first bars of *America.*

Horace listened admiringly for a time, but he had a message to deliver, so he lit on Freddy's nose and tickled the inside of his nostril with his left front foot until the pig woke up with a tremendous sneeze. Bannister gave a start and muttered something in his sleep, but didn't awake.

"Listen, Freddy," Horace said, "Jinx told me to tell you that Garble and Simon are coming up into these woods tomorrow to have a talk with the chiefs of the rebels. There's Lobo, the head of the wolf pack, and an old horse named Chester who is chief of the cows and horses who have escaped from farms. We don't know just where they are to meet, but I'm to stay with you and try to find out."

"What does Jinx want me to do?" Freddy asked. "Go to the meeting and get chewed up by wolves?"

"I guess that's up to you. He said you'd know what to do."

"Yeah, sure. When they can't think of anything, they say: 'Let Freddy do it.' But they don't ever say what."

"Well, of course, if you don't know where the meeting is, you can't do anything. But it's up at the western end of the lake somewhere. You wait here. I'll be back this afternoon." And he buzzed off.

"The worst of it is, he really will find out where it is," Freddy thought. And of course he did. Around two o'clock he was back. "It was a cinch, Freddy," he said. "The woods are full of animals, and they were all moving one way. I picked up a little here and a little there, and the meeting is at a cave under a cliff—I can take you right there. He'll be there at nine o'clock—

with Simon, the Leader, they call him. Some
call him the Dictator. Garble is the Prime Min-
ister. Sort of the power behind the throne, I
gather.''

Freddy thought for a minute. "He'll come
in a car," he said. "Up the road that goes north
past the west end of the lake. What's the near-
est point on the road to the cave?"

"There's a little beach where the road swings
closest to the lake," said Horace. "A couple of
hundred yards in from the beach is the cliff.
He'll park by the beach."

"Fine," said the pig. "I'll need you later,
Horace, but right now I wish you'd go back to
the farm and—you know that wasp, Jacob?
Bring him back with you, and all his family and
friends. Tell him I need him badly. Make it as
strong as you want to—matter of life and
death."

Horace returned with the wasps before noon.
"You got me just in time, Freddy," Jacob said.
"We were just starting off to the convention of
the A.O.F.I.W., the Ancient Order of Free and
Independent Wasps. It's in Elmira this year.
We always have a lot of fun, but to tell you the
truth I won't be sorry to miss it. We used to
leave the kids at home, but now they're bigger

we have to take 'em, and it's just too much,
Freddy, I'm telling you. If you need help, I
figure we'd better stay home and help you.
What's the pitch?"

Freddy told them his plan, which he had already talked over with Mr. Camphor and Bannister, and then with the Indians, who had
agreed to help—indeed, had refused to be left
out.

Right after lunch, Freddy and Bannister car-
ried their canoe up and hid it in the bushes, then
hid the paddles at some distance. This was good
woods practice: anyone finding the canoe, if
they really needed to use it, could cut a young
spruce and make paddles from it; otherwise,
they wouldn't take the trouble. Then they
packed up and, led by the Indians, started for
the Indian village. Jacob and his family—there
were about thirty of them—rode on Freddy's
coonskin hat. They yelled and laughed and sang
songs all the way; it was pretty trying for
Freddy, who never knew when some young
smart aleck of a wasp might not slide down onto his nose and sting him, just out of sheer high
spirits.

They had supper at the village, and then all
piled into two old cars and jounced west for sev-

eral miles over a wood road that presently turned south, acquired a black top, and ran down past the west end of the lake. After half a mile, they saw on their left a beach of fine yellow sand. At the south end of the beach, they drove the cars off the road and hid them. Then they sat quietly and waited.

Freddy did not plan to go up to the cave. It was too dangerous, for he was sure to be discovered. However, the Indians, who knew the cave, told him that it consisted of several rooms, from the largest of which a sort of natural chimney went up to an opening on the hillside above. Two of the best trackers volunteered to go up to that opening and listen to the meeting. They were sure they could hear nearly everything that was said.

After they had left, the others settled down to wait. The light gradually drained out of the sky, and as it grew darker, they were aware of movement all about them in the forest—unusual movement: the clumsy thump and smash of iron-shod hoofs, the swish of branches pushed aside by some large animal, the click of horns striking low-lying limbs. Several beavers came swimming down the lake, got out on the sand beach, and crossed the road into the woods. Two bears sauntered up the road, and after them came a long tan shape—it was getting dark now under the western wall of woods —but Freddy was sure it was a panther.

Gradually the sounds died away. Freddy was sure that by now the audience was all assembled in the cave. And then up the road came a car. It pulled off on to the beach and Mr. Garble got out with a loud-speaker box under his arm, and half a dozen rats hopped out after him, and followed him up into the woods.

It was nearly two hours later when Jacob, who had gone to the meeting with the two Indians, came back. "Meeting's breaking up," he said. "Garble'll be along any minute."

Freddy's first plan had been to hide in the back seat of the Garble car, and to rise up, and fall upon Mr. Garble when they were a safe distance down the road. But if the rats climbed into the back seat, he would certainly be discovered. So he had one of the Indian cars drive a couple of hundred yards up the road, and the other car the same distance down the road; then they turned around. And when Mr. Garble came out of the woods, carrying the loud-speaker, and got into his car, and started to drive home, both cars turned on their headlights and came slowly towards him up the middle of the road. And when Garble, cut off both front and rear, stopped and tooted his horn impatiently, Freddy stepped up to the side of the car.

"Kindly step out of the car, Mr. Garble," he said.

But Mr. Garble didn't. He whipped out a pistol and presented it at Freddy's nose. "One side, pig," he said. "And tell your friends to let me by."

Simon sat up on the seat beside Mr. Garble, rubbing his forepaws together. "Well, upon my soul," he said, "if it isn't my silly old comrade, Freddy. Somehow, I felt that we might have a reunion this summer. Truly, a festive occasion. Let us celebrate it with fireworks. Pull the trigger, Mr. Garble," he said savagely.

"I really wouldn't, Mr. Garble, sir," said Bannister, who had popped up at the other window with an even larger pistol which he pointed at the man.

Mr. Garble lowered his gun, but kept it pointed at the pig. "It seems to be a stand-off," he said. "Suppose we just both put away our guns and go quietly home."

"I've got a better idea," Freddy said. "O.K., Jake." And at that, the wasps rose in a swarm

"One side, pig," he said, "and tell your friends to
let me by."

from his hat and went for Mr. Garble and Simon.

Simon was lucky. He and the other rats
jumped from the car and scuttled off into the
woods. But Mr. Garble couldn't get out quickly,
because Freddy was holding the door. He
yelped and shrieked, and finally ended up
crouched on the floor with his coat over his
head, before Freddy called the wasps off.

He had some trouble calling them off.
"Have a heart, Freddy," said Jacob. "This is
more fun than twenty conventions. Darn it, I
bet I bent my sting on his collarbone that time."

But Freddy was firm. "I just want to kidnap
him," he said; "I don't want him sick in bed."
He knew that wasps are not cruel by nature;
they just take pride in good workmanship. For
a wasp, to sink his sting in a tender spot and
make his victim yell, is the same as for a ball-
player to hit a homer. I don't suppose they
ever think how it hurts.

So the wasps went back on Freddy's hat, and
then Garble moved to one side and Freddy slid
under the wheel and drove back to the Indian
village, followed by the two carloads of Indians. They put Mr. Garble in a room in one of
the cabins for the night, but they didn't lock
the door or tie him up. They left six wasps on

guard. They thought that would be enough to keep him safe. Then they took the loud-speaker and smashed it up with an ax.

CHAPTER

11

The day after the meeting in the cave the revolutionists began the raids. It was the time which historians of the revolt now call the Reign of Terror. Cars were stopped and overturned all over the county; farmers, starting out to do their morning chores, were driven back into the house; cows refused to come in at milking time; several barns were set fire to. In Centerboro, cats were insolent to their mistresses, horses went out of their way to insult people on the street, a car with a black dog at the wheel roared up Main Street and knocked over several pedestrians. A rabble of cows and horses galloped through the business section, overturning trash cans and smashing windows. Dr. Wintersip was chased up a telephone pole by a hitherto quite inoffensive little dog named Sweetie-Pie.

Warnings that this sort of thing would take place had been printed in both the *Bean Home News* and the Centerboro *Guardian*. Nobody paid much attention to them until the outrages began. But now people became alarmed. There was a mass meeting which passed resolutions demanding that the state police restore order. But there wasn't much the troopers could do. They arrested a horse for kicking in the door of a feed store, and a number of dogs for various offenses, but as these animals had no money for fines, and as there was no animal jail, they were just released with a warning.

Quietly, a few farms were taken over. A committee of animals would call on the farmer and explain that they were taking over, that the farm work would be done just as before, but that one of their number was now boss from whom the farmer would take orders. Sometimes the farmer was allowed to remain in the house if he agreed, in other cases he was compelled to live in the barn. If he put up a fight he was forcibly ejected.

Simon hated the Beans and their animals, and consequently it was he who headed the committee that called on Mr. Bean. Probably the rat had some doubt about Jinx's good faith, for he insisted that the cat take charge of the interview. In consequence, Jinx had no chance to explain his position secretly to the farmer, and Mr. Bean was naturally very angry at him. "You miserable critter," he said; "why, you're lower than these rats. After all, they're acting according to their nature, which is mean and nasty; but you—pah! I've no words for such a wretched traitor. What's your opinion, Mrs. B.?"

Mrs. Bean wrinkled up her eyes and considered the cat, who did indeed look wretched. Instead of the rather cocky attitude which was usual with him, he had a sheepish look, and he could not meet her gaze. Even his fur looked bedraggled.

"I don't know what to say, Mr. B., and that's the truth," she said. "When I think of the times he's sat on my lap, purring while I stroked his fur—and of the saucers of cream I've given him—I just can't understand it." And then when Jinx shot a quick look at her, she deliberately winked at him.

"Well I know what to say," Mr. Bean returned. "I say get out of this kitchen and stay out! Don't ever come in here again."

"Now, Mr. Bean," said Simon, sitting up and rubbing his forepaws together, "let us not be hasty. Surely you see that our friend Jinx is doing the very best he can for you. He remembers, I am sure, your many kindnesses in the past, and is desirous of repaying them by befriending you during these troubled times."

"He could best repay us by breaking your neck," said the farmer.

"Tut, tut; such violent language!" said the rat with an oily smile. "Let us have no insults, I beg. Or I might find it necessary to invite my friends in." He waved towards the window, outside which two tough and rangy-looking cows were peering in. "They would be only too happy to overturn your cookstove, and I presume there is a fire in it? Yes. And then what becomes of your pretty house? No, I think we can arrange things on a friendly basis. Eh, Jinx?"

"Eh?" said Jinx. "Oh . . . yes." Then added with an attempt at great firmness: "We'll stand no nonsense, Mr. and Mrs. Bean."

"Excellent!" said Simon. "And furthermore . . . ? Eh—continue, Jinx."

"And furthermore," said Jinx rather wildly, "while you will be allowed to remain in the house, you will obey my orders in everything. All the hay and grain and food will be in my charge. I will occupy the guest room, and will—"

"Why, you—!" Mr. Bean jumped to his feet and reached for the lid lifter on the stove. But Mrs. Bean was ahead of him. She pushed him aside. "None of that, Mr. B.," she said firmly, and scowled at him with such ferocity that he sank back, puzzled, in his chair.

"Now, Jinx," she went on, "suppose you come up and show me just how you want the guest room fixed up for you." She looked at him meaningly. "I remember there were some things about it you didn't like, and as you are being so good as to let us stay in the house, I'd like to have everything satisfactory."

They went up the stairs together as they had hundreds of times in the past. Simon and Mr. Bean both looked after them doubtfully. Then Simon said: "I am glad that Mrs. Bean takes this so well. I realize that it will be a great change for you both, but—"

"Oh, shut up!" said Mr. Bean.

Up in the guest room, Mrs. Bean closed the door, then got a broom from the closet. Jinx darted under the bed, but she only laughed. "No, Jinx," she said. "I know what you're up to. Now screech for all you're worth." And she began whacking the mattress with the broom. So Jinx gave it all he had. You could have heard him up at the duck pond.

The two cows came up on the back porch and looked in the screen door, but before Simon could call them in, the cat came tearing down the front stairs and with another despairing shriek shoved the door open and ran off.

Mr. Bean's laugh fizzled behind his whiskers like a damp firecracker. Mrs. Bean came downstairs, dusting off her hands. "I guess that settled *him*," she said.

Simon followed the cat out rather hastily but in the doorway he turned. "I'm afraid you don't take us very seriously, ma'am," he said. "You may find your mistake when your house is burned down. But we will give you one more chance; we'll be back presently."

And indeed they were back an hour later, accompanied by two big gray wolves.

Mr. Bean went out on the porch to talk to them. He had a shotgun under his arm which he kept leveled at the wolves.

This time Jinx didn't say anything. He knew that Mrs. Bean would have told Mr. Bean that he was really on their side, and he was afraid that if he talked very big, Mr. Bean would get to laughing and give the show away.

Simon made no attempt to be conciliating. He said: "Jinx has persuaded me to give you one more chance. As you quite well know, Bean, I have only contempt for you and your silly animals. And we'll have no more big talk from you. You'll do as you're told. You'll carry out Jinx's orders as if they were mine. Any insubordination will be promptly punished.

"And in case you think you can get away with anything, I will warn you that there are a dozen more wolves who are eager and anxious for trouble. Obey, and there'll be no damage done. But don't get it into your head that you can make a fort out of this house and stand us off with that gun. We won't need to attack you; we

"Mr. Bean had a shotgun under his arm which he leveled at the wolves."

will simply lay siege to you and starve you out.
For you'll have to go out some time to get more
food, and it will then be an easy matter for
these boys to pick you off.''

Mr. Bean realized the truth of this. He knew
that standing a siege wasn't possible. The animals could even cut off the water, which came
down in a pipe from a spring above the house.
All they had to do was rip up the pipe. He half
raised the gun, and his finger twitched on the
trigger. Then without a word, he turned and
stomped into the house.

Jinx came in with him. Mr. Bean watched
through the window until Simon and his bodyguard had taken themselves off, then he said:
''Well, cat, I hope you're satisfied. What are
your orders for the day?''

''Now, now, Mr. B.,'' said Mrs. Bean, ''what
Jinx has done, he's done all for the best. All
he's tried to do is protect us.''

''And get to sleep on the guest-room bed,''
Mr. Bean put in.

''Please understand me, Mr. Bean,'' said the
cat. ''I don't want to sleep anywhere but in my
regular place, on my pillow, back of the stove.
When the rat offered me this job, I had to decide quick, and I said yes because I thought I
could make things easier for you, and for my

friends. Maybe I decided wrong. I'm getting a lot of criticism and hard looks from those friends, I can tell you. I haven't dared to tell them why I did it. Though a few of them have enough faith in me to guess why, I think."

"I apologize, Jinx," said Mr. Bean. "I ought to have guessed, I expect. You've always been a good cat. But what are we going to do?"

"I don't know. It doesn't seem to me that the revolt can be successful. The trouble is, we loyal animals aren't organized. And if we were, we couldn't fight wolves and wild cows and panthers. But I'm going to talk to some of the animals, and maybe we can do something."

Even though most of the Bean animals were loyal, Jinx didn't feel that he could take the chance of telling them why he had taken the job of bossing the farm. The four mice, who lived in a cigar box under the stove, had of course heard his talk with the Beans, and when he went into the cowbarn, he found that the cows had guessed the truth. "We won't give you away, Jinx," Mrs. Wiggins said. "Charles was in here a little while ago and we all talked awful about you." She laughed her comfortable laugh. "It's funny, you can think up meaner things to say about somebody you really like than about someone you haven't got any use for. By the way, Jinx, I rolled up the old flag of the F.A.R. and hid it under that box. There's still a lot of animals that would rally around it if we hoisted it, you know."

"We'll hoist it at the right time," said the cat. "But that time isn't yet."

His reception in the loft over the stable was rather different. Charles and Henrietta and their twenty-seven children had taken refuge there from the wolves. Oddly enough, though it was usually Charles that did most of the talking, Henrietta was the one who now had most to say. "Ho!" she exclaimed, "here's Jinx the rat lover. Never did I think to see the day when Jinx would clasp paws with a shabby contemptible sneak like Simon. You snake in the grass, you rat in cat's clothing, get out of this loft. It makes me sick to breathe the same air."

"Oh come, Henrietta," said the cat. "You know why I did it. To protect Mr. and Mrs. Bean and you chickens and Freddy and the rest of them. You want the house burned and the Beans driven into exile and you and your family eaten by wolves? That's what will happen if I don't run this farm for the rebels. When this is all over, everything will be turned back to the Beans and will be just as it was before."

This was perfectly true, but Jinx didn't ex-

pect—or even very much want—the hen to believe it. For if the truth got to Simon, it would
be too bad for all of them. Their safety de-
pended on Simon's trust that Jinx had betrayed
his friends.

Fortunately, Henrietta always believed the
worst of everyone. "Fine talk!" she said. She
pointed a claw at the cat. "Look at him, children. Look at a vile ignominious blackguard. A
false-hearted lying scoundrel. A dirty grovel-
ing—"

"Oh dry up, hen," said Jinx angrily. He was
mad, and after all, you can't blame him. He
thought, and I agree with him, that an old
friend like Henrietta might have had a little
more faith in him. "Now let me tell *you* something. You're moving out of here up to the pig
pen. Right away. Our Leader wants this loft for
an office. Come on. Pack up."

"The pig pen!" Charles exclaimed. "Good
heavens, we won't get a wink of sleep there with
Freddy up half the night banging on that typewriter, and snoring like a sawmill the other
half."

"You'll get a good long sleep if Simon and
his bodyguard of wolves finds you here when
he comes back. Come on—it's orders."

Charles didn't say any more.

Downstairs, Hank, the old white horse, said: "Jinx, it don't seem right, it don't seem right at all, you going over to these rats. Goin' back on your old friends, seems like. Did I hear you say there'd be wolves comin' in and out the barn? Wolves! I don't like wolves. Make me feel kind of twitchy."

Jinx could have trusted Hank with the truth, but he didn't want to speak in front of the chickens. "They won't bother you," he said. "See you later, Hank. Come on, Charles, get a move on."

CHAPTER

12

For several days, the revolutionists had everything their own way. More than fifty farms in the Centerboro district were taken over. The Camphor estate was seized and turned into a sort of concentration camp for farmers who refused to bow to the new authority. The commit-

tee, unable to escape in time, were made prisoners, and although they complained bitterly,
and in sentences hundreds of words long, were
compelled to give in.

Centerboro had not yet been taken over, and
here and there a farmer had resisted, and being
well provisioned and having his water supply
in a well close to the house, was able to hold
out. But these wells, unless actually inside the
house, had to be guarded twenty-four hours a
day, for Simon had had bags of salt dropped
down several of them at night, and their owners had had to surrender.

Even those farmers who felt that they could
hold out were forced, one by one, to surrender,
for food supplies began to give out. Simon and
Mr. Garble had planned well. Vegetable gar-
dens were rooted up by bands of roving pigs,
and fields of grain were systematically trampled by the cattle. Overturned cars on all the
roads made road blocks that brought traffic to
a standstill, and no food trucks were getting
through. Freddy saw that soon the farmers
would all be forced into the towns, and then
starved out of the towns into the cities—for of
course the farms wouldn't be producing any
more. He didn't see what the humans could do.
Send out the army against the animals? But the

army would have to be fed, and before it could get under way, the food supply would be disorganized.

Through Mr. Pomeroy and the A.B.I., Freddy was kept well informed of what was going on. He had sent word of the capture of Mr. Garble to Mr. Dimsey, and the Centerboro *Guardian* came out with an extra, splashing the news in headlines across the front page.

"GARBLE CAPTURED
Second in Command of Animal Revolt Incarcerated.

"Herbert Garble, of 184 Sherman Street, this city, was captured two nights ago by loyal forces, and is in custody at an unspecified location. Mr. Garble, formerly for a time editor of this paper, is reliably asserted to be second in command of the animal revolutionists who are currently threatening our liberties. He is alleged to be the brains behind Simon the Dictator, a rat whose history was related in our last issue.

"It is said that the $500 reported as stolen from Senator Blunder was found on Mr. Garble's person. Also, two unironed handkerchiefs belonging to Mr. W. F. Bean, which were stolen from the Bean clothesline some days ago."

An editorial at the foot of the page said: *"It is hinted that Mr. Garble may be in some bodily danger, as a band of Indians living north of Otesaraga Lake, incensed by his action in bringing wolves into their territory, are said to have sworn vengeance. Should these Indians visit their resentment upon Garble by removing his scalp or otherwise discommoding him, it seems unlikely to us that the authorities would take notice of the action by legal steps to punish them. Mr. Garble has placed himself outside the law."*

Freddy had written the editorial, and at the same time, he had had Mr. Dimsey print a poster. It was the kind of poster usually printed up in Centerboro to announce an auction or a dance or a bake sale, but only one copy was printed. And the day after Mr. Garble was shown the *Guardian* extra, Freddy had it under his arm when he made his daily call on him.

Mr. Garble was by this time pretty discouraged. At first, he had shouted and raved, begged and threatened. But the Indians paid no more attention than if he was a piece of furniture. The wasps did, though. If he looked out of the window, a wasp flew down from the ceiling and lit on the back of his neck. If he laid a hand on the doorknob, a wasp dropped to his wrist. The first night, he got up some time after midnight and crept to the window. With a pen-knife, he was starting to pry at the sash when he thought a thorn had been driven into the lobe of his ear, and a tiny voice said: "Back to the feathers, brother, if you don't want your ears pinned back. We've got the pins all ready."

When Freddy came in with the poster under his arm, Garble started to demand to be re-leased, but suddenly he stopped and pointed to the poster. "What's that? It has my name on it!"

Freddy held it out. It read:

"GRAND WAR DANCE AND SCALPING PARTY
OTESARAGA VILLAGE, JULY 18TH

3 P.M.

Following war dance, Mr. Herbert Garble, now Public Enemy No. 1, who was captured last Friday, will be

BURNED AT THE STAKE.

(stake and firewood furnished by Gilman Lumber Co.)

Admission 50¢, children half price.

Supper will be served after the entertainment by the ladies of the First Presbyterian Church of Centerboro."

"Ha, ha!" said Mr. Garble uncertainly. "You have a great sense of humor, pig."

Freddy said: "I'm glad you can see it that way. I admit that I can't feel that you'll really get much fun out of it. Old Wiggling Snake— he's the chief—is very keen for it. The Indians don't make much money out of their baskets and stuff, and we're going to have a big crowd. Going to get posters up in Centerboro, Tushville, Nineveh Falls—every village within forty miles, as well as Rome, Utica, and Syracuse."

"Look here, Freddy," said Mr. Garble. "You're not—you can't really be serious about this business? You going to have me burned in effigy or something?"

"Oh dear me, no. No, no; you couldn't get any kind of a crowd out for that. I'm sorry, you know, in a way. If you'd only behaved yourself and not turned into a human rat, it wouldn't be necessary. But at least you'll be doing some good to somebody for a change. The Indians should take in nearly a thousand dollars. And they'll have some fun, too."

Mr. Garble jumped out of his chair so agitatedly that the two wasps on guard flew down to his neck and stood there waiting with poised stings. "But Freddy," he stammered, "you—

you . . . Oh no, I don't believe you. The police wouldn't let you do a thing like that."

"You don't understand, Mr. Garble,"
Freddy said. "You're an outlaw. There's a reward of a thousand dollars for your capture.
But if you're burned at the stake, the town won't
have to pay the reward. You don't suppose
they're going to be mad at the Indians for sav-
ing them all that money, do you?"

"Bu—but you can't—you simply *can't* do such
a thing to me," the man gabbled. "Oh dear,
how did I ever get into this thing anyway?
Look, Freddy; you can get me out of it. What
can I do to get out of it? Tell me; I'll do anything. Burned at the stake! Ugh!" He shuddered.

"I don't know that I can do anything,"
Freddy said thoughtfully. "To withdraw the
plans for the entertainment now—well, I
don't like to disappoint the Indians. And what
will you do for me in exchange, if I do manage
it?"

As they had talked, Mr. Garble's eyes kept
turning to the poster, and each time he read
"burned at the stake," he shuddered. By now
he was in a cold sweat, and Freddy decided that
he had got him where he wanted him. Maybe

he didn't quite believe that he would be burned, but he wasn't eager to take the chance.

"I might," Freddy said, "I just barely might get you out of it if you did just as I told you."

"I'll do anything, Freddy—anything." Mr. Garble's teeth were chattering now. "Only, get me out of this. Burned at the stake!" he whispered. And then he fell on his knees. "Don't let 'em do it, Freddy; don't let 'em!"

"Get up!" said Freddy shortly. "And sit quiet till I get back. I'm going to see what we can do."

Half an hour later, he was back with pencil and paper. "I want you to write a note I'm going to take to Simon," he said. "Now I know that he'll suspect it, and I suppose you've got some secret password so that he'll know if it is O.K. Right?"

"Yes, we have a password."

"Good," said Freddy. "Then see that you get it in. Because if he suspects, and doesn't do what you tell him to—look, they're putting up the stake now!" And he pointed to the window, through which they could see two Indians digging a hole in the open space which was surrounded by the houses of the village. A post about eight feet long was lying beside the hole.

Mr. Garble wrote as Freddy dictated, making at the end a secret mark under his signature.

Back at the farm, Simon had not for long been satisfied with the loft over the stable as a headquarters and audience room. Guarded by two huge wolves, he had demanded and obtained the use of the front parlor in the house. Here, seated in a handsome red plush chair, directly under the picture of Washington Crossing the Delaware, he received Jinx and Freddy later the same day.

They stood in front of him and Jinx raised his paw. "Hail, our Leader!" he said. "I have brought another volunteer who wishes to join us."

Simon grinned. "Dear, dear," he said. "And who is this stout gentleman? A new recruit, I think you said? He will indeed be a weighty addition to our forces. That is, if we can afford to feed him. Eh, boys?" He snickered, and the two wolves laughed obediently.

"You know me, Simon," Freddy said. "And I know you. I don't like you any better than I ever did, but I am an animal, and if it comes to a showdown between animals and humans, I am on the animals' side. Also, I think you have the winning team, and I like to be on the winning side, myself."

"Very shrewd of you," said the rat. "And you expect, I suppose, to be rewarded for these bluff and straightforward sentiments by a position of high trust in the new government. Tut, tut, my dear friend; old Simon is a silly old fellow and has a trusting nature, but do you know —he is not inclined to believe you. And what do you think of that?"

"I think you're missing a bet. I've got some influence among the animals around here. If I throw it your way, it's going to save you a lot of trouble."

Simon's beady black eyes shifted from Freddy to Jinx and back again. "And how about the good Beans? Do you agree with Jinx that they have had their own way on this farm long enough?"

"I don't want them to come to harm," Freddy replied. "But it is time for a change. Jinx will run the farm as well as Mr. Bean did, and I am sure he will be as thoughtful for his old masters as they were for him."

Rats are not loyal, and do not understand loyalty. That Freddy should stay loyal to Mr. Bean, when it was to his advantage to go over to the other side, was something that Simon found it difficult to believe. And so he was not hard to

They stood in front of Simon and Jinx raised his paw.

convince that Freddy would betray old friends for a more comfortable position.

"Very well," he said. "We'll take you on as assistant to Jinx. But no tricks! Poor old Simon may be easy to fool, but remember that these boys will be keeping an eye on you. Eh, boys?" he said to the wolves, who showed their teeth in what may have been meant as a smile, but made Freddy feel very plump and pink and edible.

Jinx again raised his right paw. "Our Leader, hail!" he said. "I am the bearer of a letter to you from Honorable Garble." And he produced the letter that Freddy had dictated.

Simon opened and read it. "Ha," he said; "so he has escaped from the Indians! And you and Freddy assisted him? Excellent. You have our thanks." And he bowed slightly and looked more kindly at Freddy.

Then he referred again to the letter. "He wishes us to meet him at the Camphor house to-morrow afternoon. He feels—and I cannot but agree with him—that this parlor is not sufficiently magnificent for the Leader of a great animal republic. He wishes us to take over the Camphor mansion as our executive palace. The drawing room, if I remember it correctly, would be suitable for a—dear me, I suppose we should call it a throne room. He says that he will have it prepared for us.

"Not, you understand," he added hastily, "that old Simon cares for such pomp and splendor. But we must remember the effect on our subjects, eh? Yes, I think this idea of Mr. Garble's is excellent."

"Splendid, my Leader," Jinx exclaimed, and Freddy and he both saluted. "Highly fitting, your Magnificence," the pig added.

"Tut, tut," said Simon, "no flattery, if you please. Grand titles are not for simple old Simon. Simon is your leader, true, but he is also just a plain citizen." But Freddy could see that he was pleased. And he thought: We've got him; we've got him through his vanity. "As your Excellency pleases," he said, and backed, bowing, to the door. And Jinx, taking the hint, backed, bowing, beside him.

CHAPTER 13

The country around Centerboro, and indeed through much of the state, was in a bad way. Up in the Indian village, Freddy had not actually realized how far the revolution had gone. But when they started for Centerboro in Wiggling Snake's car, he became pretty frightened.

They saw several abandoned cars, and by them, the shoulders of the pavement and the ditches were cut up by the hoofs of animals. Farther on, they came round a curve and a flock of sheep jammed the space between the fences. Beyond the sheep, a small truck stood in the middle of the road. Some of the sheep faced around and glared menacingly at Mr. Camphor and Bannister. Bannister muttered: "I wish we didn't have those lamb chops in the freezer, sir."

But Jinx hopped out, and the sheep made way for him. A man stuck his head out of the truck and shouted: "Hey, what's the matter with these critters? They been trying to climb in here and bite me."

"Better turn around and go back," said Jinx.

The man started to say something else, and then he said: "Holy smoke, look at that!" And pointed across the fields.

A man was standing on a rock in the middle of a hayfield and laying about him with a hoe. Around him, the grass kept moving, and now and then small brownish animals came into sight as they leaped up towards him.

"Rabbits, by cramps!" yelled the man in the truck. He jammed on the accelerator and, knocking aside one or two sheep, backed around and roared off down the road.

At one place, a mob of cows was shoving stones and dirt and fence rails on to the pavement to make a road block, and they had to detour through the fields. And then they came to a farm owned by a man named Coombs. A big herd of cows was milling about the house, and several of them, led by a huge bull, were trying to break down the back door. They were butting it and pounding it with their hoofs. And then around the corner of the house came a collie. He didn't waste any time barking. He went for those cows, driving them, nipping at their legs, dodging when they tried to hook him. In a few minutes, he had them herded and headed for the barn. The bull faced him for a moment, bellowing and pawing the ground, but the dog gave two or three sharp barks and the bull suddenly turned tail and ran for the barn.

"Good gracious," said Freddy, "did you see that? Those cows were actually scared to death of that dog. If they'd ganged up on him, they could have hooked and trampled him and driven him off."

"They've been trained for generations to run from dogs," said Wiggling Snake. "Even though they know they're stronger, they're afraid."

"I wonder how many of the dogs are loyal," said Freddy thoughtfully.

"Most of them," said the Indian. "They've been trained in the same way."

"Golly," Freddy said, "that gives me an idea. I believe I know how we can break this revolution. We've got Garble. Now if we can capture Simon, all these cows are our chief problem, and I know how to lick that."

"How about the wolves?" Mr. Camphor asked. Still in his war paint, he looked more like an Indian than the Indians themselves.

Freddy said: "The chief tells me that if we can get rid of the leaders of the revolt, it will be easy to drive the wolves back where they came from."

"That's right," Wiggling Snake said. "Wolves are cowards. Even a pack of a dozen will run from a man with a gun. You leave the wolves to us. You know, summer people will pay good prices for wolf skins."

"People have been brought up on stories about the big bad wolf," said Running Deer, "but actually the big bad wolf is a sneaking hen-house robber. Simon knows that; he's got the wolves for window dressing. Strictly for shudders."

In Centerboro, Freddy bought some pieces of heavy wire mesh at the hardware store, and then got a friend of his, a Mr. Smith, a plumber, to bring certain equipment out to Mr. Camphor's. There, Mr. Smith welded the wire mesh into a sort of cage that fitted under the seat and between the legs of the armchair that stood at the head of Mr. Camphor's dining-room table. The lid of the cage opened inward, like the leaves of a double door when you pulled a string.

They cut out the bottom of the armchair so that anyone sitting in it sat directly on the lid of the cage, and then they took it into the big drawing room and draped it like a throne, with a red plush curtain. In the meantime, Mr. Camphor had gone up into the attic and found some gold paper, which he cut into the shape of a crown.

The preparations were only barely ready when one of the wasps left on guard at the gate came and reported that Simon and Ezra, with two wolves, were just coming in the gate.

Besides the committee and Miss Anguish, there were half a dozen refugee farmers in the house. Freddy seated them in chairs around the other end of the room, and warned them to be as quiet as possible. There was silence for several minutes, then the door opened and Jinx entered, followed by two huge wolves, and then by Simon and his eldest son, Ezra. Jinx walked backward, bowing at every other step. When he reached the throne, he stood aside and motioned towards it.

"Will your Excellency," he said solemnly, "deign to be seated?"

Simon paused. He looked round—at the solemn farmers, at the puzzled committee, at the Indians who filed in and closed the door behind them.

"Who are these people?" he demanded, indicating the latter.

"Your very loyal subjects, your Excellency," said Jinx. "They only wish to ask to be allowed to live in peace in the forest, as they always have."

"We will take up their case later," said Simon. "Is Mr. Garble here?"

"Mr. Garble seems to have been delayed," said the cat. "We expect him any minute. In the meantime may we proceed, your Excellency, to the little ceremony which we have prepared? Freddy—"

Freddy stepped forward. He was carrying the gold paper crown. "Your Eminence—" he began.

But Simon brushed the crown aside with a snarl. "What are you trying to do—make a monkey of me?" he demanded. Then remembering that he was after all a dictator over a great number of subjects, he said: "You forget, I think, that although I am your leader, I am still a plain citizen, and I like plain titles. All this pomp and ceremony—"

"Forgive me, Excellency," said Freddy, "but in ruling a nation, pomp and ceremony are necessary. The ruler of an empire is not, and cannot be, a plain citizen. He must submit to being placed on a pedestal, to being seated on a throne. Only thus can he receive the proper respect, the honor which his followers delight to give him." And stepping forward quickly, he pressed the gold paper crown firmly down on Simon's head.

The rat sensed that Freddy was making fun of him, but all the bowing and scraping and flattery had tickled his vanity, and in spite of himself, he was very pleased. And then Freddy whispered to him. "You've got to put on the dog," murmured the pig. "Your subjects want a king to act like a king. Come on; here's a chance to make an impression. Make a speech. Pass a couple of laws."

"Maybe you're right," said the rat, and

Freddy could see that he was anxious to be convinced. Then he got up into the chair, trying to look as kingly and ferocious as he could. "Friends and loyal subjects," he began—and then Freddy pulled the string, there was a click, and with an alarmed squeak, Simon vanished.

For a minute, there was complete silence in the room.

"Dear me," said Miss Anguish, "what an amusing trick!"

Then as an angry chattering broke out under the folds of curtain beneath the chair, the two wolves made a dive for Freddy. But the pig stood his ground. "Take it easy, boys," he said, and pointed towards the door. Two of the Indians had slipped out and now popped back in again, holding guns. At the sight of firearms, the wolves dashed for the window and leaped through, taking the screen with them. Ezra scrambled after them. And Freddy went up to the chair and pulled off the red curtain, revealing Simon, imprisoned in the small cage.

Simon was practically foaming with rage, but Freddy paid no attention to his remarks. "Ladies and gentlemen," said the pig, "let me present to you that noble figure, that magnificent conqueror, Simon the Dictator. Come on, Simon, speak to the gentlemen, and stop that silly chattering. Let us hear and tremble at your imperial squeak."

Simon controlled himself with difficulty. "I don't know what good you think this is going to do you," he snarled. "Let me out of here or you'll regret it, pig."

"Sorry, old boy," Freddy replied. "I guess you'll just have to stay there till your revolution goes pop. Bannister, will you get a chair to stand on and hang that cage up on the chandelier?" So the butler stood on a chair and hung the cage on the chandelier.

Although he was only a rat, the farmers and the committee members were afraid of Simon, or at least of the power he had over all the other animals. But when he was safely hung in his cage from the chandelier, they began to laugh at his threats. Freddy and Jinx didn't laugh as hard as the others. They knew Simon for a tough and wily old scoundrel. If he were to escape, they knew that he would have no mercy on those who had imprisoned and ridiculed him.

They knew too that it wouldn't be as easy to break him down as it had Mr. Garble. He was too smart. He wouldn't be fooled by any threats of burning at the stake. But Freddy had an idea, and after consulting with his friends,

The butler stood on the chair and hung the cage to the chandelier.

he spoke to Simon. "We don't quite know what to do with you, Simon, old Excellency. A sea voyage would probably be the thing, to calm you down and settle your nerves. We can't, of course, arrange that for you, but we can provide you with an imitation which will have, we hope, much the same effect." And taking hold of the string that hung down from the cage, he set it swinging gently. "We hope, of course, that you are not subject to seasickness."

Simon held out longer than they expected. The to-and-fro motion didn't seem to bother him much, and he went right on swearing at them and threatening until Bannister climbed up on the chair and set the cage spinning as it swung. The combination of motions was too much for the rat. His voice got weaker and weaker, and then he lay down on the bottom of the cage and closed his eyes. But at last, he gave in.

"Stop it!" he moaned. "Stop it and I'll do anything you want."

"Right now we don't want you to do anything but just stay here and be Dictator, your Excellency," said Freddy. "Bannister can come in every half hour or so and give you a few swings, so you won't be bored."

"What good does it do you to torture me?"

Simon said. "You can't stop the revolution by keeping me prisoner. It's gone too far. Zeke and Ezra and the rest of the rats will carry on, and with Mr. Garble to advise them—"

"Mr. Garble isn't advising anybody," said Freddy. "He's still a prisoner. No, your jolly old Majesty, just take it easy and enjoy the voyage. Bannister, I think the ocean is becoming a little too calm."

So before they left, Bannister gave the cage another swing.

CHAPTER

14

To the consternation of Freddy and Jinx, the imprisonment of Simon and Mr. Garble had little effect on the course of the revolution, which spun along under its own steam. The newspapers published the story of Simon's capture, but Ezra proclaimed himself dictator in his father's place, and farm after farm continued to be taken over without resistance. The Governor had a regiment of soldiers sent into the area, but there wasn't anybody to shoot at; only animals grazing quietly in the fields. The wolves faded off into the woods, and the other animals refrained from violent acts while the soldiers were in the vicinity. There was nothing for them to do.

The Camphor house was in a state of siege. The Indians stayed on and their guns kept the wolves at a distance, but such supplies as were needed had to be fetched from Centerboro under armed convoy. Fortunately, there was a large quantity of food stored in the house. The committee wanted to get back to their homes, but there was no way of taking them there. They had finally run out of funny stories, and this made them cross and snappish, as there was nothing else to talk about. Only Miss Anguish seemed to be enjoying herself; she read and crocheted, and spent a good deal of time talking with Simon, where he hung from the drawing-room chandelier. He tried every way he could think of to get round her and persuade her to set him free, but she always managed to refuse on some pretext or other.

Freddy and Jinx had not been mentioned in

the newspaper stories of the capture of Simon, and they were consequently free to move about the country without being challenged. Ezra had made several speeches from the Grimby cellar hole, but he was a poor speaker and with no microphone to increase the sound of his voice, the enthusiasm of his followers had definitely fallen off. It was this that encouraged Jinx and Freddy to persuade Mr. Camphor to go down under armed guard one evening and make a speech giving the human point of view. Ezra was to speak that night, but the Indians and the Bean animals drove him and his guards away, and then Mr. Camphor stood at the top of the cellar steps and spoke.

"Fellow animals," he said, "—for remember that, though a man, I too am an animal—I have come to speak to you tonight because there are two sides to every question, and so far, only one side has been presented to you. Simon has ably presented the side which believes that the animals should take over. I wish to present the side which believes that men should be left in charge.

"This does not mean that I believe animals should have no hand in running things. I will take that up a little later. For the moment, let us consider what will happen in a world run by Simon the Dictator.

"In the first place, paws and hoofs cannot be used in many operations which are necessary on a farm—in running machinery and so on. Men will have to be kept on to do all this work—which now they do willingly. But will they do it well or willingly if they are under the orders of a cat or a horse? Men will have to be slaves, and there will be hatred between men and animals, as always between masters and slaves. Will life be as pleasant for either men or animals under those circumstances?

"Again, Simon has told you that you will live in the houses and the men will occupy the barns. I don't believe any horse or cow wants to live in a house, any more than any man wants to live in a barn. Every animal likes to live in the type of structure which is built for him. Men in houses, cows in barns, horses in stables."

Mr. Camphor developed this idea at some length, as you can do for yourself if you have the patience. Then he went on to remark that Simon had much to say about slavery. But the relationship between men and animals was a partnership, he said, not slavery. Cows were free to wander about the pastures; they did no work. Horses worked, but their hours were not long; they were simply doing their share of the work that produced food for both them and the farmer. Dogs were sometimes tied up, but only when they were cross and might bite somebody.

The animals listened in silence. Now and then, there was a buzz of agreement. The audience seemed to be composed mostly of farm animals; no wolves were in evidence, and Jinx reported that he could find only a few of the gaunt hill cattle and horses from the north.

When he had spoken for some time, Mr. Camphor said: "Many of you, I suppose, support Simon because you feel that in our present form of government, animals have no vote. But if you believe that under a dictator you will have some say in the government, you are making a great mistake. There will be one party: Simon's. If you vote at all, you will vote for Simon. There will be nobody else to vote for. You will have no freedom of choice and very little of action. You will be worse off than you are now.

"Apparently, you have the choice between being slaves to a rat, or what some call slaves to humans. This is a bad situation. But there is a cure for it. I can tell you what it is in three words: Votes for animals!"

There was some scattered applause at this, and Mr. Camphor went on to talk, as he had to the committee, about what he called "full representation." He said nothing about being a candidate for governor, but stated that he intended to use his influence to have a bill presented in the next legislature admitting animals to the vote. And this, he asserted, would be far better than having the animals take over under a dictatorship. "Animals must govern *with* men," he said. "It is no more fair for animals to have all the power than it is for men to have it."

There was a good deal of applause at the end of the speech, and it was plain that Mr. Camphor had made a good impression. "Fine campaign speech, Mr. Camphor," said Jinx. "Give the men as good as you give the animals and you're cinch for the governor's chair next fall."

"But you ought to have told them who you are, and that you're a candidate," said Freddy, with a wink at Jinx. "If you can get the Senator to jam that animal suffrage bill through before election, you'll have the biggest plurality in history."

"Good gracious!" Mr. Camphor exclaimed. "I don't want to be governor." He thought for a moment. "Or do I?" he said. "You know, if I thought they'd always applaud, it would be kind of fun. But what does a governor *do*, Freddy? I don't know the first thing about it."

"Oh, he just signs bills and opens poultry shows and has his picture taken. I should think you'd get a kick out of it, Jimson. You make a dandy speech. And you've got the committee if you get stuck."

"It's always kind of scared me," Mr. Camphor said. "At first I thought it would be nice, but then I got worried, and that's why I tried to get out of it. But I don't know—maybe I'd enjoy it at that."

"You really wanted to be governor all the time, I think," said Freddy. "Naturally, you were nervous about it. But I tell you, Jimson: if you go out and stump the state for votes for animals, in no time at all, you'll be the best known politician in the country. Goodness' sakes, you might even get to be president. President Camphor! Wouldn't that be something?"

Freddy realized that the applause had gone to Mr. Camphor's head. The pig was sure that he still really didn't want to be governor. But if he made a lot of speeches in favor of animal suffrage, it would turn a great many animals against Simon. That was the important thing now. But he decided not to say any more about it for a while.

They had left their car on the back road, with an armed Indian to guard it, and after the meeting, Mr. Camphor drove Freddy and Jinx down to the Bean farm, then left for the Indian village. The house was dark. It was too late to report to the Beans, so the two friends went up to the pig pen. The door was locked, and they had to hammer on it for some time before a quavering voice said: "Who—who's there?"

"It's me—Freddy," said the pig. "Come on, Charles, open up."

"I—I don't think I can move this bolt," said the rooster. "It seems to be stuck."

"If you moved it to bolt it, you can move it to unbolt it," Freddy replied. "Come on, we want to get to bed."

"Who's we?" Charles asked.

"We is us," Jinx said. "And for your information, rooster, my claws are half an inch long and if you don't open up in three seconds, the first time I catch you in the open, they'll pull your wings off. You want to go through the rest of your life as Charles, the Wingless Wonder, hey?"

"Yeah?" said Charles. "Well how do I know who you are—come banging on the door in the middle of the night. I've a good mind to just let you stay there.''

"Listen, Charles,'' said Freddy. "Want me to prove who I am? Remember the time we were talking, and I was congratulating you on what a fine wife you had in Henrietta, and you said: 'Oh sure, she's a good wife, but that's because I trained her. She used to try to run things,' you said, 'but after I slapped her down a few times and showed her who was boss—' ''

Charles interrupted with a sharp squawk. "Ouch, Henrietta!'' he squealed. "Quit! Freddy's lying; I never said any such thing.'' There was a flutter of wings and more squawks; evidently, Charles was getting his ears soundly boxed.

Freddy called: "Open up or I'll tell the rest of it,'' and at that, the bolt was quickly pulled back and the door opened.

"Let him alone, Henrietta,'' said the pig, for the hen was still taking occasional swings at her husband. "Charles didn't say that; I made it up to make him let me in.''

"Maybe you said it so he'd let you in,'' Henrietta said, "but that doesn't mean you made it up. The big blowhard! It sounds just like him!'' And she took another swipe at her husband's head with her claw.

Evidently Charles was getting his ears soundly boxed.

The twenty-seven chickens, ranged on improvised perches along one wall of the pig pen, paid little attention to the disturbance; evidently, they were used to hearing their father get scolded. Even when Freddy turned on the light, only a few of them pulled their heads out from under their wings, and recognizing the familiar faces of the newcomers, tucked them back again.

While Henrietta was still clucking indignantly at her husband, Freddy went over to his typewriter and looked at a piece of paper on which someone had started to write something. "I, Charles, rooster of this parish," he read, "being of sound mind and not crazy or anything, do hereby declare this to be my last will and testament. To my beloved wife, Henrietta, I leave—" Here the typing stopped.

Jinx had come over and read the paper too. He and Freddy grinned at each other, and then the cat turned to Charles. "Been making your will, eh, rooster? How about leaving me a couple of million?"

"I ought to leave you a dose of poison," said Charles. "Anybody that would go back on Mr. Bean the way you did! Anyway, what's so funny about making my will? With these wolves around here, what chance have I got? They'll eat me sooner or later."

"Well, they'll eat Henrietta too, then. So what's the good of leaving anything to her? Better leave it to somebody that can enjoy it. Like me."

"You feel that it is foolish of me to attempt to provide for my family?" Charles asked stiffly.

"Not if you've got anything to provide with," said the cat. "But I bet that's why you stopped writing your will where you did: you couldn't think of anything to leave 'em."

"I could too!" Charles snapped. "I've got— well, I've got money in the First Animal Bank."

"Eighteen cents—you told me so yourself when I wanted you to go to the movies a couple weeks ago. Give or take a nickel—I suppose you may have picked up a few cents since then. Eighteen cents and a bunch of tail feathers— that's what your estate will amount to, old boy."

"Oh, quit picking on him, Jinx," said Freddy.

"Heck, I'm just advising him," said Jinx. "If he wants to leave his tail feathers to Henrietta, it's all right with me. I don't suppose anybody will contest the will."

"Let's get some sleep," said the pig. "I've got things to do in the morning."

But instead of going to bed, he sat down in front of the typewriter, rolled in a sheet in place of Charles's unfinished will, and began thoughtfully pecking away at the keys. This is what he wrote. And if you ask me why, at this time and place, he wrote it, don't expect me to explain the working of a poet's mind.

Thoughts on Teeth

The teeth are thirty-two in number.
You'd think so many would encumber
The mouth, but they fit neatly in
Below the nose, above the chin,
Behind the lips, a double row,
So strong and sharp, and white as snow.

To keep them shining, clean and bright,
You scrub them morning, noon and night.

The teeth are used in chewing steaks
And pickled pears and angel cakes—
A list of all the things they chew
Would reach from here to Timbuctoo.

O think of all the tons of food
Which in your life your teeth have chewed!

Though birds lack teeth and cannot chew
Their victuals up like me and you,
Gizzards, it's generally conceded,
Do all the chewing that is needed.
A gizzard no cause for discontent is:
Birds never need to see the dentist.

The use of toothpicks is thought rude
And should in public be eschewed.

To animals, both pigs and men,
Teeth only seem important when
They're not around. If you have not
Got 'em, you miss them quite a lot.

So keep your teeth, don't let them go;
Replacements cost a lot of dough.

CHAPTER

15

Freddy found it hard to tell whether the revolution was losing or gaining ground. Reports of the A.B.I. seemed to show that half of the farms in the county were in the hands of the animals; but deprived of the big voice that had kept up their resentment against humans, the animals had certainly become milder. No more houses had been burned, and there was little of the rioting that had marked the first days of the revolt. If it had not been for the wolves, and for the gangs of wild cattle who patrolled the countryside, Freddy felt that with the help of the dogs, things could be quieted down.

For in most cases, the dogs had remained faithful to their masters. They rounded up the cows and drove them into the barns every night, and often broke up meetings which they felt might cause trouble. Of course, they couldn't tackle the wolves, since being cow dogs, they worked singly and not in packs; and they hesitated to try driving the tough northern cattle.

Mr. Camphor's speech on votes for animals, too, had made a favorable impression. Most animals figured that if they got the vote, and could have some say in how the country would be governed, they would be better off than they would under a dictator. A number of them sent word secretly to Freddy that they didn't like the new way of doing things, and that if he had any idea of leading them back to the old way, they would be with him. Most of the animals living on the Bean farm, with the exception of some of the rabbits and woodchucks and others who had been influenced by Simon's inflammatory speeches, were still loyal.

The morning after Mr. Camphor's speech,
Freddy and Jinx had a talk with Robert, the
collie, and the little brown dog, Georgie. Then
all four of them went up and had a talk with
Mr. Schermerhorn's dog, Johnny, and Mr.
Witherspoon's Spot, and Mr. Macy's Shep.
And then they went down to see Mr. J. J. Pomeroy, and had him send out twenty bumblebee
operatives of the A.B.I to invite all the dogs
within a radius of fifteen miles to a mass meeting at the Grimby house that night.

There must have been four hundred dogs at
the meeting. Freddy did not address them himself; he had Robert do it, since he felt that a
meeting of dogs should be addressed by a dog.
Also, Robert was known and respected throughout the countryside.

A sliver of new moon was setting in the west
when Robert stepped up onto the top cellar
step. "Friends and fellow canines," he said, and
all across the clearing, he could see hundreds of
tails slowly wagging. From that moment, he
knew that he had his audience with him.

He began with some discussion of the traditional friendship between dog and man.
The dog, he said, was man's elder brother. He

guarded and watched over him; no other animal so had man's trust and liking. Their relationship was founded on mutual affection. And so on.

On the other hand, Robert went on, the dog and the rat were natural enemies. The dog was straightforward, trusting, and reliable; the rat was dishonest, sneaky, and disloyal. Simon, who had set himself up to be dictator over an animal empire, was no exception. "If we accept his rule," Robert said, "we will lose that which we value most, our freedom. In place of affection, there will be suspicion; in place of kindness, cruelty; in place of trust, hypocrisy.

"Now, my friends, many of us have felt hopeless in the face of these dark days that have fallen upon us. Many of our friends have gone over to the side of the revolutionists; our masters have been driven from their homes or shut up in them like prisoners. I cannot speak for other animals, but I think that few dogs look forward with any confidence to a life under a dictator. The novelty of the idea that the animals can take over is, I think, the reason why it has been taken up so enthusiastically by many of our neighbors. Looked at more closely, the idea is completely unsound.

"But what can we do? Singly, my friends,

nothing! But look about you. In this clearing about the Grimby house tonight, there are enough of us, were we but banded together, to drive wolves and cattle and horses back to where they came from. And to keep them there. To bring back the good old times that we long for, and to keep them here. My friends, what do you say, shall we bring them back?"

The wagging tails in the clearing were like a wind-tossed lake, and the dogs barked frantic applause. When it had died down, Robert said: "My proposal is that we form into regiments of a hundred dogs each. You realize that this will be military service; those of you who have the job of protecting a farm or a home will have to give up that job while you are on duty. But if we do organize, and stick to our duty, I don't think it will be long before we can all go home."

Dogs have a good sense of discipline. Before the meeting broke up, there were four regiments organized and standing to attention under Robert, Shep, and two wise old cow dogs from Dutch Flats, Hughie and Bosco. The regiments were to alternate service every two days, but two were to be on duty at all times, one at headquarters, the Bean farm, the other on patrol duty.

As soon as Ezra learned of these new developments, he divided his forces into two groups, one based on the cellar of the Grimby house, the other on the cave. Now his patrols, which had been in the habit of going out by threes and fours to keep order among the farms which he controlled, had to go out by twenties, and even this wasn't enough if a patrol ran into one of the dog regiments. For even one cow dog could handle a dozen cows, and though few single dogs were a match for a wolf, a hundred dogs could make mincemeat of a small wolf pack.

But neither dogs nor wolves believed this until it came to a trial. Freddy was up on the back road with the First Regiment. He was riding his bicycle, as he frequently did when he went out with the dogs. Some of the bumblebees of the A.B.I. had brought word that there were two patrols in the neighborhood; one had just left Schermerhorn's where there had been a report that Mr. Schermerhorn had shot at a wolf the previous night, and to punish him for this, he had been ordered to sleep in the barn and wash at the pump from now on. Both patrols were moving towards the Bean farm.

From where Freddy stood, the ground sloped away sharply to the south. Down the slope, his own pig pen and the chicken house were visible, though the rest of the Bean buildings were shut from view by the trees of Mr. Bean's woods. On the other side of the road was the Big Woods. As he watched, half a dozen wolves trotted out into the open space around the pig pen, sat down, lifted their muzzles in the air, and began to howl.

"My gosh," said Freddy, "they're after the chickens! Look, Robert, there come some horses and a couple of those tough cows. They're backing up to kick the door in! Robert, we must do something!"

"Don't see what we can do," the collie replied. "We can't tackle those wolves. We could drive the horses and cattle all right, but those wolves will tear us to pieces. What could poor little Georgie do against a wolf?"

Freddy looked around at the dogs who were lying about at the side of the road or sniffing about in the brush. "You're almost as big as a wolf, Robert," he said, "and so are half these dogs. If half a dozen poor little Georgies—beagles and cockers and fox terriers—are on the other end of your wolf, I should think you could manage him all right. Darn it, look! they're starting on the door. By George, if you won't order a charge, I'll go down and tackle them alone." And he got astride his bicycle, which was pointed downhill at the edge of the road, and put a foot on the pedal.

The dogs had heard him and crowded about him to look. Whether he would really have charged alone down the slope to the rescue of his friends is open to some doubt. What happened was that his foot slipped, gave a strong push on the pedal, and the next thing he knew, he was careering down the hill. His yell of dismay must have been taken by the dogs as the order to charge, for within seconds, they were bounding along beside him—matching bound for bound, for the ground was hummocky and uneven and it was a miracle that he managed to keep to the saddle, or rather to come back down on it after each tremendous bound.

Faster and faster the ground whizzed by, and as his speed increased, the noses of the leading dogs fell back. By the time he reached the pig pen, he was a good three lengths in the lead, and he was having less and less contact with the saddle of his bicycle. Fortunately, when the bicycle finally crashed head-on into a long-horned cow, Freddy was not on it. He was in the middle of a bound, a good two feet above the saddle. Consequently, he was above the cow; he flew right over her and knocked the wind out of a wolf.

He scrambled to his feet; the wolf was out cold, and the cow was still entangled with the bicycle; but all around him was a leaping, snarling, snapping whirlpool of wolves and dogs and cows. Freddy thought he had better get into it. A wolf's hind leg went by; he grabbed it and crunched.

A pig's teeth are sharp and he has a lot of them. That crunch was no joke. The wolf twisted around and tried to slash Freddy, but Freddy shook him out straight and crunched harder; and after trying this a few times, the wolf gave in. "Leggo," he said. "I quit. I give in."

Freddy was so astonished at having won a fight with a wolf that for a moment he just hung on.

"Hey, quit it," said the wolf. "I said I gave up. What do you want—to chew that leg right off me?"

So Freddy let go and the wolf limped off and lay down in the shade of the pig pen and panted.

The fight was going badly for the revolutionists. The cows and horses had had their ankles

He flew right over her and knocked the wind out of a wolf.

nipped unmercifully, and when they turned to threaten their tormentors with hoofs or horns, other dogs started nipping and driving them. One little dog was from Centerboro—he was a beagle named Sweetie-Pie who belonged to Mrs. Lafayette Bingle, and who in the early days of the revolution had chased Dr. Wintersip up a tree—this Sweetie-Pie was so good at it that after the fight he was appointed Captain in Charge of Cows, and a few months later left Mrs. Bingle and took a job as cow dog on a big farm in the south of the county. Now the cows were in full retreat, and the wolves too were trying to pull out of the fight.

And, suddenly, the dogs found that there wasn't anybody to fight. Except for half a dozen wolves who had been bitten up and were too exhausted to run, and the cow who had got entangled with Freddy's bicycle, the enemy was gone. And then the door of the pig pen opened and Charles strutted out.

"Well fought, lads," he said. "Well fought indeed! It is to my deep regret that I could not give you a hand, for the bolt stuck again and I could not get the door open. But though un-happily it was not I who led you on to victory, my hearty thanks to you, one and all."

Sweetie-Pie turned from the rooster to Robert. "Who's this cannibal?" he asked.

"My good sir," said Charles pompously, "your ignorance regarding my name and—er, accomplishments is perhaps to be excused on the ground that you are a stranger to this part of the country. I am Charles. Does that satisfy you?"

"It's no more than I expected," said the dog darkly. And then with sudden ferocity, he shouted: "My name is Sweetie-Pie; you want to make something of it?"

Charles started back in alarm. "Make something? I fail to see what one could make—that is, no, it's a very pretty name. Your owner must be very fond of you to call you such a pretty name."

"Fond of me!" Sweetie-Pie shrieked. "I'm the worst-tempered dog in Centerboro! I chase bicycles and bite postmen and pick on cats! So would you if you had a name like that. Laugh, why don't you? Laugh and see what happens to those tail feathers."

Charles was like most stupid people, he was not stupid all the time. He had occasional flashes of common sense, and even of brilliance. He had one now. He saw clearly why

Sweetie-Pie was bad-tempered, and he said: "Yes, I guess I would. But you can change your name, can't you? What's the matter with Fritz? Or Tige? They're good names."

"Sure they are. But how could I change when everybody on the block calls me Sweetie-Pie?"

But Charles was tired of the dog's troubles, and besides he wanted to make a speech before the regiment drifted away again. "I guess that's your problem," he said, and hopped up on the garden chair beside the door.

"Friends and noble rescuers," he began, "on behalf of my dear wife, my twenty-seven innocent children, and myself, I wish to tender you my heartfelt thanks and gratitude—" But after the first perfunctory cheer, the animals turned to discussing what should be done with the prisoners, and they paid no more attention to Charles. So I don't know why we should either.

CHAPTER

16

Most of the animals who had besieged the pig
pen had run away but the dogs had rounded up
half a dozen cows, and there were as many
wolves who were too exhausted to run. "If we
let 'em go," Freddy said, "we'll just have to
fight 'em all over again. I bet Mr. Camphor

would let us have his garage and stable—it's a big place and built of stone. Make a swell prison. Come on, you wolves. Up on your legs. We're going for a walk."

It took them two hours to get to Mr. Camphor's. None of the wolves was seriously injured; they were worn-out rather than badly bitten; and the cows had had their ankles nipped until they had to hobble. As they stumbled through the gate, Mr. Camphor and his guests came out on the terrace to meet them.

"Goodness me," said Mr. Camphor, "look at all the dogs. You going hunting, Freddy?"

"We've been," said the pig, and explained.

Mr. Camphor said, of course, they could use the garage. "I'd like to move Simon out there too. We're pretty sick of his raving and threatening and calling names, and the only way we can stop him is to make him seasick—and that's sort of cruel. Out there, he can talk his head off, and we'll let his friends suffer."

But when they went into the drawing room, Simon was gone, cage and all.

Nobody knew anything about it. Nobody had been in the room that morning; most of Mr. Camphor's involuntary guests avoided it, since they were tired of the rat's mingled threats and pleadings. Only Miss Anguish spent some time there; she said he was such an interesting conversationalist. But, of course, nobody could ever figure out what her idea of conversation was.

Freddy at first was inclined to suspect Miss Anguish. He thought that if in exchange for helping him to escape, Simon had promised her a high position in the new government, she might have released him. Or he might have promised her a new car; or a canary in a cage. There was no telling what kind of a bribe might have taken her fancy. But, presently, he had news that turned his suspicions in another direction.

Jacob and the five wasps who had been left to guard Mr. Garble came flying in to report that their prisoner had escaped. "We ought to have guessed what he was up to, Freddy. He had a pocketful of these cigars he smokes—I don't know the name of 'em and don't want to, they smell like burning rubber even before he lights 'em. Well, he started to smoke six of 'em at once—lit 'em all and then took a couple of fast puffs on each one. Boy, what a smell!

"We didn't do anything; if he wanted to poison himself, it was O.K. with us. But pretty soon, we began to get kind of groggy ourselves. And by then, it was too late. We passed out,

Freddy. And when we came to—no Garble, no cigars, nothing but an awful smell. He'd forced up the window and got away.

"Gosh, Freddy, I'm awful sorry. But who could have suspected anything like that?"

"Nobody," Freddy said. "You weren't to blame. He just outsmarted us. He probably got in touch with Ezra or Zeke and came up here and cut Simon down. Anybody could walk in after all the folks had gone to bed. We ought to have had a guard on him."

For the next few days, nothing was heard of Mr. Garble and Simon. Mr. Garble would not have dared return to Mrs. Underdunk's, where he made his home, for a warrant was out for his arrest on the charge of attempting to overthrow the government. The order was out, too, to shoot Simon at sight. In the meantime, animals and farmers fought a guerrilla warfare over the countryside; farms were freed, and retaken; the Macy farm changed hands five times in one night. But whenever one of the dog regiments met a band of the wild northern horses and cattle, it was the dogs who won. And nearly all the wolves had disappeared. That one fight at the pig pen had been enough for them. Freddy felt sure that it was organizing the loyal dogs that had broken the back of the revolution.

Every day, more of the domestic animals, who in the first days had enthusiastically joined the revolutionists, gave themselves up and asked to be taken back by their human masters. Even the rabbits, now that they were no longer kept continually stirred up by Simon's speeches at the Grimby house, began to think that the dictatorship of a rat wasn't going to be much of an improvement on their old way of life. A number of them threw stones at Jinx—who they, of course, supposed was still managing the Bean farm for Simon.

If it was the fight with the dogs which had discouraged the wolves, and to a lesser extent the tough northern cows and horses, it was the "votes for animals" movement which had influenced many of the animals from local farms to abandon the revolutionists and return to their homes. A very short experience under a dictatorship had shown them how little freedom they could expect, and the thought of being able to vote for a candidate of their own choosing was very pleasing to them. Several delegations called secretly on Mr. Camphor and pledged their aid in case he should run for governor.

But although farms had been liberated, not all the exiled farmers had returned to their homes, and many farms were still run by the rebel animals. Jinx no longer pretended to run the Bean farm; now that Simon and Mr. Garble had escaped, both he and Freddy had been unmasked, and knew that their lives were in danger. For bands of revolutionists still roamed the countryside, and the A.B.I. reported that there were still heavy concentrations of the enemy in the woods to the west of the lake.

One evening after supper, Freddy was sitting at his typewriter in the pig pen, deep in composition of a poem entitled *The Charge of the Dog Brigade*. This effusion was to commemorate the famous fight at the pig pen, and more particularly, of course, Freddy's gallant leadership of the charge. For he had very prudently told nobody that it was a slip of the foot, and not a sudden gallant and fearless impulse, that had started him charging down that hill in the teeth of the enemy.

> *Half a field, half a field,*
> *Half a field onward,*
> *Down to brave Freddy's pen*
> *Tore the one hundred.*
> *"Forward the Dog Brigade!*
> *Charge!" gallant Freddy said.*

Into the valley of death
  Rode the one hundred.

Wolves to the right of them,
Cows to the left of them,
Horses in front of them
  Hollered and thundered;
Struck at with iron shoes,
Yelled at with howls and moos,
Into the jaws of death
  Charged the one hundred.

He had got this far when, at a light tap on the door, he looked out of the window. Charles and his family were walking around outside, guarded by two dogs. And in front of the door stood Mr. Camphor and Miss Anguish.

"Oh gosh," Freddy said, "they would come when the place isn't picked up!"

Jinx was curled up on the bed. He got up, stretched, and joined Freddy at the window. "When would that be?" he asked. "To my knowledge, that piece of string has been on the floor in the same place since last Christmas when you unwrapped your presents. Anyway, who is it? Your window's so dirty I can't see."

"I like it that way," said Freddy. "Makes it

more interesting, speculating. But I think I hear Mr. Camphor's voice."

"Well, for Pete's sake, let him in!" exclaimed the cat. "You can't pick up this place in two minutes. Take more like two years. Oh, all right," he said, as Freddy still hesitated; "I'll let 'em in myself." And he went to the door and flung it open. "Enter, sir and lady," he said, with a deep bow. "Enter the poet's lair. See the poet himself at work, hammering out the hexameters, enshrining in deathless verse his own two-cent exploits, his eye in fine frenzy rolling —nay, practically popping out of his head in self-admiration—"

"Oh, shut up, cat," said Freddy. "How do you do, Miss Anguish. Hello, Jimson. Wish I'd known you were coming, I'd have picked up a little. I've had the chickens staying with me this week and the place is in rather a mess."

"Thought maybe you and Jinx had been having a pillow fight," said Mr. Camphor, and Miss Anguish said: "Oh, dear me, Dr. Hopper, I'm so glad you didn't pick up! It's nice to see your place just as you live in it. As another great poet sings: 'It takes a heap o' livin' to make a house a mess.' " She fluttered about, looking at everything. "And this is you, isn't it?" she asked, stopping at a snapshot of Hank, hitched

He went to the door and flung it wide open.

to the buggy. "Younger, I suppose. You're rather slimmer."

Freddy started to explain, but she had fluttered on and was looking out the window. "And this lovely picture window. What a charming view!"

The window was small and the view so distorted by the crinkly panes and so dimmed by dust and cobwebs that you couldn't recognize anybody through it if they came close and peered in at you. Freddy liked it for that reason; he said his friends looked more interesting and—some of them—handsomer, when seen through it. He explained this to Miss Anguish, who for once seemed to agree; she said: "And all those little creatures walking around out there. Are they supposed to be chickens? There's one with four legs. And—how interesting—there's another with two—no, three—heads. Dear me!"

Mr. Camphor said; "If those chickens are staying with you, I suppose they'll be coming in to go to bed pretty soon. It's after eight. I guess we'd better be going. Miss Anguish was anxious to see your little house—"

"I'd heard so much about it," said that lady. "Quite, quite charming! And to see you actually in the throes of composition—turning out

one of your lovely poems! I wonder," she fluttered; "would you make just a tiny one for me?
Just for me alone?"

"My goodness," said Freddy, "I don't know.
I never . . ." He was very much flattered. "I
wonder," he thought. "What rhymes with 'An-
guish'—'languish?' No. How about 'Lydia?'
Let's see. Lydia's hideous—oh, golly! But wait."
Then aloud, he said:

> *"In comparison with Miss Lydia's*
> *All other faces are hideous."*

Miss Anguish clapped her hands with delight. "How sweet! Such a pretty compliment!
Oh I can't tell you how—" She broke off, for
outside there was a sudden outburst of flapping
and squawking, and then a heavy knock at the
door. "Open up, pig," called Mr. Garble's
voice. "We know you're in there."

CHAPTER
17

Jinx ran to the window. It was beginning to get dark, but he could make out a mob of animals —cows and horses. "We can't escape," he said. "We'll have to open up. Too bad the dogs aren't here. You know where they are, Freddy?"

"Two regiments, Bosco's and Robert's, have

been mopping up to the east, north of Centerboro. They plan to make a sweep south of the
lake and then up around the west end and drive
the cattle up through the woods back where
they came from. Look, Jinx; Garble doesn't
know you're here. Go in the other room and get
into the wig drawer. Curl up and cover your
nose and your paws and if he searches, he'll
think you're a black wig. Then you can get
away and warn the dogs."

It was the sensible thing to do and Jinx did
it. Then Freddy opened the door. And immediately as Mr. Garble, with a pistol in his hand,
entered the pig pen, Miss Anguish gave a loud
scream and threw her arms around his neck.
"Oh, save me, save me!" she wailed. "Save me,
my noble deliverer, from these terrible kidnappers!"

Unfortunately, Mr. Garble was prepared for
something of the kind. He swung her aside and
kept the pistol trained on Freddy and Mr. Camphor, so that they didn't dare make a rush at
him.

"Save me and take me back to my brother,
Judge Anguish. He will repay you well," she
went on. And then she gave a scream and, let-
ting go of Mr. Garble, climbed up into
Freddy's easy chair, holding her skirts tight

around her, as Simon, with Zeke and Ezra and half a dozen of his children and grandchildren, came in.

Simon showed his long yellow teeth in a malicious smile. "No cause for alarm, ma'am," he said. "Old Simon wouldn't hurt a fly."

"Well, I'm not a fly," she quavered. "And I don't like rats, either."

"Maybe when you're better acquainted with us, you'll like us better," said Simon. "You'll find me a kindly old fellow, ma'am. Old Simon the Dictator. Dear, dear; it's the ex-Dictator now, I'm afraid. Yes, Freddy, old friend, we're pulling out. Your side has won, for the time being. So make the most of it while you can. When your friend Camphor here gets his votes for animals through—well, suppose old Simon runs against him on the animal ticket. Eh? Governor Simon—how does that sound?"

"Nauseating," said Freddy.

Simon's whiskers twitched angrily, but he controlled himself. "Dear, dear; such a fearless pig! Eh, Mr. Garble?"

"You talk too much, Simon," said Mr. Garble shortly. He frowned at them for a moment, then he said: "We're taking you all with us. We had intended to capture only the pig, but I think we will hold you all to ransom, since we are fortunate enough to find you here."

He turned to Miss Anguish. "Did I understand you to say that these people had kidnapped you? If so, we have rather turned the tables on them, haven't we?"

Miss Anguish rushed at him again but he held her off. "Oh, I knew you would help me!" she cried. "You have such a kind face!"

"Wow!" said Freddy, and even Simon looked startled.

"I will help you if you will help me," said Mr. Garble. "I'll be frank with you, ma'am, and with you, Mr. Camphor. I need money. Now that our scheme to have the animals take over has broken down, there is a warrant out for my arrest, and I've got to get out of the country. I suppose your brother, Miss Anguish, will pay five thousand dollars for your release? Mr. Camphor also can no doubt arrange to have that amount conveyed to me. As for the pig—"

"I haven't got any five thousand dollars," said Freddy.

"Perhaps Mr. Bean would think you were worth that much," said Mr. Garble. "Though I am inclined to doubt it. However, should he not be inclined to ransom you, we shall have to find another way of disposing of you," he added with a mean smile.

There was a silence while they looked at one another hopelessly. Then Miss Anguish said: "Oh, thank you, thank you! I knew you would take me away from these terrible people. Take me back now, and my brother will be only too glad to pay you whatever you ask."

"I'm afraid it isn't as simple as that," said Mr. Garble. "If I take you back to him right away, he might feel that I wanted too large a reward. He might even call the police and accuse *me* of kidnapping, instead of these other gentlemen. No, I think we'll just take you to a safe place and release you when we have the money.

"But we're wasting time. Kindly come along." And he turned towards the door.

"Wait a minute," Freddy said. "If we're going to be away for some time, I'd like to pack a bag. And Mr. Camphor—he hasn't even a toothbrush. I want to put in a few things for him."

Mr. Garble said all right, but to hurry up, and Freddy went into the other room. He got out an old carpetbag of Mr. Bean's, and then he looked in the wig drawer. "Quick!" he whispered. "Into this bag, Jinx!" And the cat jumped in and Freddy snapped it shut.

The bag with Jinx in it was heavier than it looked, and Freddy had to pretend to swing it as he came out into the other room. Mr. Garble drove them out of the front door at the point of the pistol. Mr. Camphor's car was just outside; he had driven it straight up the hill from the barnyard. At an order from Mr. Garble, the cows and horses trotted off up the hill.

"Mr. Camphor will drive," said Mr. Garble. "In beside him, pig." Then he and Miss Anguish and the rats got in the back seat. And when they were out on the road: "You know where my sister's house is? Drive there. I should tell you," he added, "that my sister is away and will know nothing about my holding you for ransom, so that when you are released, it will be useless to have her arrested."

Now that Jinx had heard where they were going, Freddy wished that he could let the cat escape. Thus the dogs could be warned and there would be a chance for a rescue. But the bag was in the back seat.

They drove into Centerboro and, by back streets, to Mrs. Underdunk's house. This was a big old-fashioned brick house with steep pitched slate roof. With the pistol at their backs, they were marched through the kitchen door and down the cellar stairs. Freddy remembered that cellar, and not with pleasure. He and Bloody Mike had been locked in the jam closet, as has been told elsewhere. They had managed to escape, but Freddy didn't see how he was going to manage to escape a second time. He didn't see how he was going to raise the ransom money either. He'd be nailed up in a crate again and shipped off to Mr. Garble's uncle in Montana. Indeed, in a dark corner of the cellar he saw the selfsame crate that a year or so ago he had only at the last moment been released from. There were the labels on it: "Mr. Orville P. Garble, Twin Buttes, Mont.," and, "Fragile. Do not Crush." This time he'd really go.

Mr. Garble got pen and paper and had Miss Anguish write a note to her brother, stating that she was held prisoner, and would be released when $5000 was brought to the Grimby house at midnight three days later. A similar note was written by Mr. Camphor to his aunt, who was spending the summer at Lakeside.

"You want to write a note to Mr. Bean, pig?" Mr. Garble asked.

"No," said Freddy. "Mr. Bean can't raise that kind of money, and I wouldn't want him to if

"Into this bag, Jinx!"

he could. Not for me. But I've got $50 in the First Animal Bank. If you want to let me go, I'll go right out there and get it and bring it back to you. I'll promise to go and come right back without saying a word to anybody." But to himself, he said: "I could write a message on a piece of paper."

He didn't really expect Mr. Garble to fall for this, and Mr. Garble didn't. "I guess we won't put such a strain on your honesty," he said. "I wouldn't want to put temptation in your way. You might decide to telephone the sheriff or somebody, and then think how you'd hate yourself tomorrow morning. No, we mustn't let you break your word. And, in fact, I think we'll let your fifty go. I need the money all right, but it's worth fifty to me to know that you won't be around here any more. I've a long score to settle with you, pig. And there's the crate over there in the corner that'll settle it. You see, I kept it. I knew some day I'd get you back in it." He scowled vindictively at Freddy.

After a moment, he turned to the others. "Miss Anguish, I have prepared rooms for you and Mr. Camphor on the third floor. You will be quite comfortable. Both rooms are lighted by skylights—no windows—and even if you managed to get out on the roof, you could only slide down and fall twenty feet to the ground."

"Look here, Garble," said Mr. Camphor; "you can't get away with this. The police will have you twenty-four hours after we are released."

"My dear fellow," said Mr. Garble, "twenty-four hours after you are released, I will be out of the country. You will remain locked in your rooms here for several days after the money is paid. When I am safely out of the country, the sheriff will get a telegram telling him where you are."

"But your sister. I understand she's away, but—"

"She knows nothing about this," Mr. Garble interrupted. "And she can prove it. She won't be back from California until it's all over."

"All very well," said Mr. Camphor, "but the disgrace! She may have a solid brass alibi, but people are going to think she knew all about it."

"On the contrary, people are going to be very sorry for her, having a criminal for a brother. It isn't as if she'd ever been popular here, you know. If she had, people might enjoy pulling her down. No, my guess is she'll be really quite sought after."

"And where are you going to put me?" Freddy asked.

"Why, we'll let you have the run of the cellar for a day or two. Chance to get acquainted with your new home," he said, indicating the crate.

None of them could think of anything more to say, and Freddy was anxious to get the carpetbag open and consult with Jinx. To his dismay Mr. Garble picked up the bag. "I'll show you your rooms," he said, and with the pistol, motioned Miss Anguish and Mr. Camphor to precede him up the cellar stairs.

CHAPTER

18

Up in the little room with the skylight, Mr. Camphor sat down on the bed—there wasn't any chair—and considered. The five thousand dollar ransom didn't bother him—he was a rich man and would gladly have paid many times that to get out of the fix he was in. Judge Anguish too was rich; there was no need to worry about his sister. But how about Freddy? Freddy was his friend, and a friend was worth many times five thousand dollars.

"I'll tell Garble," he said to himself, "that I'll put up the five thousand for Freddy. I suppose I should have told him before, and saved Freddy the worry he's going through, but if Garble thought I would spend that kind of money on a pig, he might raise my ransom to twenty-five thousand, and I want to get out of this as cheaply as I can."

This train of thought was interrupted by a faint meow. Mr. Camphor got up. He looked under the bed, under the dresser, and in all the dresser drawers. No cat, but the meowing continued. "Funny," he thought; "it sounds almost as if it came from that carpetbag, but I never knew a toothbrush to meow before." He sat down, but as the sound continued, he got up and opened the bag. And out sprang Jinx.

"Whew!" said the cat. "Stuffy in there. I used to like the smell of mothballs but I guess I'm cured. I can see how a moth might feel about 'em. Well, what do we do now?"

"Well, if we could get out, we ought to warn the sheriff. But the only opening in the room is one pane of the skylight that slides aside. You could crawl out and maybe get on the peak of the roof. Then if you yelled, maybe somebody'd bring a ladder and get you down."

"Let's have a look."

But when Jinx got out, the pitch was too steep to be climbed. His claws wouldn't hold him on the slates.

"I guess that's that," said Mr. Camphor. "We might as well settle down and play tick-tack-toe. Got a pencil?" But neither of them had a pencil.

But Jinx caught sight of a hot-air register set in the wall. "What's this?" he asked.

Mr. Camphor explained that it was the opening of a duct that brought hot air up from the furnace in winter. "This register pulls out," he said. "Look here. But there's just this narrow oblong tin duct that goes down through the wall to the furnace. It's probably too narrow for you, and if you slid part way down and got stuck, you'd just have to stay there."

"Not if you tear up the bed sheets and make a rope, and I hang on to one end with my claws and you let me down. I don't think it's too narrow. If it is, I'll yell and you pull me up. But if it works, where do I come out?"

"You ought to come out in the cold-air duct that brings fresh air in from outdoors. It might be open; sometimes it's kept open in the summer. O.K., let's try it."

Cats can make themselves pretty thin. Although the duct wasn't much more than three inches wide, Jinx went down without sticking. He went down past the furnace into a sort of tin box, which was the intake for cold air, but there was no way out. The metal slide that could be opened to let fresh air in was shut.

He was about to give the two tugs on the bed sheets, that was to be the signal for Mr. Camphor to pull him up, when he heard voices. They seemed to be very close to him, but then he realized that they were coming down through a hot-air pipe from one of the rooms above him. These pipes were just like speaking tubes, and anyone in the furnace could hear everything that went on in the house. The voices were those of Mr. Garble and Simon.

"It's not my fault that the scheme failed," Mr. Garble was saying. "It was nobody's fault. Nobody could have foreseen that the stupid loyalty of the dogs would smash our plans."

"All very well, Mr. Garble; all very well," said Simon. "But you brought us back from Montana to take part in the scheme—*your* scheme. And now it has failed, and what are you going to do for us? You are going to run for it and leave us holding the bag. You know, Mr. Garble, it would be a very neat solution of our troubles if we were to turn state's evidence—to drop in on the sheriff this evening, say, and tell him a few things. Eh?"

"You wouldn't get much out of that," Mr. Garble replied.

"Satisfaction, Mr. Garble. The satisfaction of knowing that you, our comrade in arms, were safely and comfortably housed for the next twenty years or so. Eh?"

Mr. Garble was silent for a time, then he said: "You don't seem to realize, Simon, that I'm on the run myself. But . . ." He hesitated a moment. "But I'll tell you what I'll do. I told Camphor that as soon as the ransom was paid, I was going to skip the country. But I'm not skipping. Not for six months, when the hullabaloo will have died down and I'll have had time to grow a beard. I'm going to stay in the cave, up at the west end of Otesaraga Lake. Back of the hall where we held our meetings, there are two rooms. I just found them by chance. They open about five feet from the floor when you squeeze in behind that big stalagmite that looks like a pipe organ. Nobody will ever find you there. I've stocked them and fitted them up in the last month or two. I'm going to hide out there. And you can hide out with me, and after I leave, you can use the place. Live there. No one will ever find you if you take ordinary precautions, and you can raid nearby farms in perfect safety."

Jinx didn't wait for any more. He gave two tugs on the rope of bed sheets, and Mr. Camphor pulled him up. And then they sat up until after midnight, working out a plan of action.

At eight next morning, Mr. Camphor heard the key in his bedroom door turn, and then Mr. Garble came in. In one hand was the pistol, in the other a small tray with a cup of coffee and two slices of toast. "I'm not a very good cook," he said. "I'm afraid you'll be on short rations while you're here." He put the tray on the bed, went out, and locked the door. Mr. Camphor heard him tap on Miss Anguish's door.

When Mr. Garble had gone downstairs again, Mr. Camphor said: "I think Miss Anguish's room is next to this one, and this hot-air duct must serve both rooms. The register in her room ought to be right opposite this one." He went to the register and called softly: "Miss Anguish! Can you hear me?"

There was a pause, and then Miss Anguish's voice said: "Yes. Hello. Who's calling, please?"

"This is Mr. Camphor. I'm in the next room."

"Oh, good morning, Mr. Camphor. Nice of you to call. How've you been?"

"Er—quite well, thank you," he said. "Miss Anguish, I presume you have a bathroom with your room?"

"Oh, yes," she said; "such a pretty one, all pink and blue. And the soap is pink, too. So thoughtful of Mr. Garble!"

"Well—yes," said Mr. Camphor. "Now listen, this is what we're going to do." And he told her. "Open the pane in your skylight, and when you smell smoke, go in the bathroom and shut the door. With luck, we'll be out of here in another hour." Then, as she apparently thought he was on some kind of telephone, he said good-by; and she said: "Good-by. Oh dear, how do I hang up?"

"Just leave the register open," he said, "and go in the bathroom and shut the door. Good-by."

"Good-by," she said. "Thank you for calling."

"Gosh," Jinx said, "is she really all there?"

"Oh, I think so," said Mr. Camphor. "She just does that because it amuses her."

"Well, it doesn't amuse me," said the cat. "It makes my whiskers curl."

"Let's get going," said Mr. Camphor.

So they tore up the rest of the bedding and broke up a small bathroom chair and even the frame of a picture on the wall, and they dropped all this, and everything that was in-flammable in the room, down the hot-air duct. Then Jinx went down on his bed-sheet rope. "And be sure to pull up fast," he said. "I don't want to be broiled."

"Don't worry," said Mr. Camphor. "And here—take this newspaper. We don't want our fire to go out before it gets started."

Down in the cold-air box, Jinx built his fire. First newspapers, then the sticks of wood, then on top, leaving room for some draft, the bedding to make a good smoke. Then the match and two tugs on the rope, and Mr. Camphor drew him quickly up.

The smoke came up quickly, too—first thin blue smoke, then thick gray bad-smelling smoke from the smoldering bedding; and it poured in a thick column out of the register and out through the open pane in the skylight.

"Suppose nobody sees it," said Jinx. "Lift me up to the skylight, Mr. Camphor. I'll have

He yelled "FIRE" at the top of his lungs.

to go out and yell 'Fire!' if we want to be rescued."

So Mr. Camphor shoved him through the open pane and Jinx clung to the skylight frame and yelled "Fire!" at the top of his lungs. And the top of his lungs could be heard half a mile. In no time at all, people ran out-of-doors and threw up windows and they all yelled "Fire!" too; and in five minutes the fire department was there. They didn't get any answer when they banged on the door, so they broke five windows so they could all get in at once, and they put up ladders and broke more windows on the upper floors, and they hooked up hoses and wet the house down good. They broke a few more windows for fun and then rescued all the prisoners. But they didn't ever find out where all the smoke had come from and to this day you can always start a long argument in the Centerboro firehouse by saying: "Remember the Underdunk fire? Now where do you suppose . . . ?"

And Mr. Garble was not in the house.

CHAPTER
19

Mr. Garble's car was in his sister's garage, but Mr. Camphor's car was not in the driveway where it had been left last night. "He doesn't know that we know about the cave," said Freddy. "That's where he'll be."

"We'd better mobilize one of the dog regiments," said Mr. Camphor. "We can attack the cave. Get the sheriff to go along and take him right to jail."

The sheriff, who had come to the fire, objected. "I don't want that fellow in my jail. We've got a nice crowd there now—nice lot of boys—no murderers or kidnappers. Mostly just burglars. They don't want to associate with crooks like Garble."

"Don't you call burglars crooks?" Mr. Camphor asked.

"Why, in a way, I suppose they are," said the sheriff. "But to tell you the truth, most of 'em don't make much out of burglary, they just practice it mostly so they can get caught and sentenced to another term in my jail. More like a club, it is."

"Well," said Freddy, "maybe we can turn him over to the F.B.I. I expect that kidnapping is a federal offense, and then he'd be sentenced to a state prison—not a county jail."

This made the sheriff feel better, and he drove them up to Mr. Camphor's house. In the past two or three days, the dogs had rounded up a lot of the revolutionists, and the garage was now crammed to bursting with cows and horses; there were even a dozen or so on the top floor,

which had at first been reserved for wolves and
coyotes.

When they saw their captors looking in the
window, they all began shouting at once, beg-
ging to be let out.

"Who speaks for you?" Freddy asked, and a
big tough-looking bay horse pushed forward.
He was Chester, formerly leader of the northern horses and cattle.

"Look, mister," Chester said, "this Garble, he
said it was going to be a bloodless revolution.
What's bloodless about it? Look at my ankles,
I tell you what, pig, you let us out and we'll
promise to go back north where we came from
—all of us. I'll personally give you my word
for it. We're fed up. There's nothing for cows
and horses to eat in the woods, and if we go
out in the fields, the dogs are on us. We want
to go home."

"Your revolution's over anyway," said
Freddy. "Sure, I don't see why you shouldn't
go." And he unlocked the door.

Nearly all the cows thanked him when they
left. The wolves simply slunk out and loped off
up the lake. But Chester said: "Thanks, pal.
Ever get up around Ringtail Pond, just look me
up. We'll throw you a party." And then he too
clumped off.

So then the sheriff drove Freddy and Jinx back home. The farm was free of the rebels, and the animals all piled out to shake paws and hoofs and congratulate them on their escape. Everyone knew now that Jinx had not really gone over to Simon's party, and Henrietta in particular apologized handsomely for all the names she had called him when she'd thought him a traitor.

Mr. Pomeroy, who was getting hourly reports from the bumblebees on the mopping-up operation of the two dog regiments south of the lake, sent word for them to push on to the sand beach near the cave and wait there. "They're meeting no resistance," he said. "They'll be there in an hour. Then we can attack the cave."

"We can't use 'em to attack the cave," Freddy said. "Unless we want some of 'em to get shot. Garble has a pistol. And the door to the inner cave, he said, is five feet from the floor of the big hall. See if Jacob and his family are around, will you, J.J.?"

Fortunately the wasps were home, hard at work chewing up wood to build a new house. But like all wasps and most people, they were glad of an excuse to knock off work for a little while. "Specially as I've got a grudge against that Garble. Bent my sting on his collarbone last time we met," he said.

So they drove up and met the dogs at the sand beach, and the dogs went up and surrounded the cave while Freddy and the wasps went in. Everything went smoothly—though perhaps not for Mr. Garble. "The door's behind that big stalagmite," Freddy said, and the wasps disappeared behind it. There was a short silence, then a loud yell from Mr. Garble and a terrified squeaking from the rats, and out they all tumbled. The dogs rushed in and pounced, and in no time, they were all prisoners.

So Mr. Garble went off to prison and after a good deal of discussion, Simon and his family were piled into the crate intended for Freddy and shipped off, collect, to Mr. Garble's uncle in Montana. When they got there, Mr. Garble's uncle wouldn't accept them and pay the charges, so they were sent back to Centerboro again, and there Mrs. Underdunk wouldn't accept them and shipped them off again. They shuttled back and forth across the continent half a dozen times, and for all I know they are travelling yet.

Mr. Camphor's suggestion to do away entirely with taxes was taken up by the committee, and soon the newspapers were full of pictures of him with such headlines as: "Camphor to run on no-tax platform," "Overwhelming popularity assures Camphor victory," and "Camphor most popular candidate in history." For the general acclaim, the cheers and congratulations, that greeted his first appearance on the platform, had made him change his mind about running. "If they want me so much," he said, "then I must be the man for the job."

He did not, of course, abandon the cause of votes for animals, and when he spoke in a hall, there was always a section of seats reserved for animals, and it was always well filled. Occasionally, Freddy appeared on the same platform, pleading the cause of animal suffrage. The pig was a very convincing speaker—not eloquent, but very matter-of-fact and practical, and therefore convincing. Even then, I suppose, he had political aspirations, though it wasn't until some years later that he actually ran for office.

Although the revolt had been suppressed, there was still a good deal of discontent among the woods animals. Campers and hunters were occasionally attacked and chased. Freddy spent the rest of that summer and fall in the woods,

—and out they all tumbled.

camping out and addressing groups of wild animals wherever he could get them together, urging them to seek a political remedy for their
troubles, through votes for animals, rather than
by the use of violence. Simon, he told them,
stood for violence, and see what had happened
to him.

With strong Republican pressure, a bill au-
thorizing animal suffrage was rushed through
the state legislature, and on election day, the
Bean animals, led by Hank, carrying the flag of
the F.A.R., marched into Centerboro and voted.
And Mr. Camphor was elected governor by
some seven million plurality over the Democratic candidate, Mr. Feebler. The animal vote
was overwhelmingly Republican, and although
no separate count was kept of animal and human votes, it was estimated that some twelve
million animals voted.

Of course, after this, Freddy became a pretty
powerful political figure. He controlled the animal vote in Otesaraga County and, consequently, since there were several times as many
animals as humans, was political boss of the
county. For a number of years, however, he
resisted all attempts to persuade him to run for
office. Some of the more influential animals in
the state wanted to run him for governor, fol-

lowing Mr. Camphor. With the solid animal vote behind him, he was sure to win. But an animal, he felt, should not accept high political office, and although in the first few years of animal suffrage, there was a scattering of animal judges and mayors, Freddy fought the idea.

Also, Freddy remembered what Governor Camphor said to him on one of his frequent visits to Albany. "Darn it, Freddy," the Governor said, "there's a lot of *work* to this job!"

Like most lazy people, Freddy could work and work hard when he wanted to. But when he didn't want to—well, he just didn't want to. And he had a hunch that being governor was a full-time job. But several years later, he did run for office. He served a term as mayor of Centerboro, and it was during his administration that he solved the traffic problem which had so snarled everything up in most American cities. The Frederick Bean Traffic Plan has now been adopted in nearly every city and town in the nation. The solution was surprisingly simple: no parking within the city limits at any time. This made cars practically useless, and people gave them up and took to walking, thus improving the general health, and cutting down the cost of living. Indeed, its benefits have not been exhausted yet.

Freddy is now working on a bill to be brought up before the State Legislature, which will do away with all schools.